Chri

CW01647945

To Father,

Hope this will help you recollect some of your own stories.

Peter & Doreen.

A PARCEL OF 'OL CRAMS

A PARCEL OF OL' CRAMS

Jan Stewer
(Albert J. Coles)

ALAN SUTTON
1980

Alan Sutton Publishing Limited
17a Brunswick Road
Gloucester, GL1 1HG

First published 1930. This edition
published 1980 by arrangement with
the copyright holders.

British Library Cataloguing in Publication Data

Stewer, Jan
A Parcel of ol' crams.
I. Title
823'.9'1F

ISBN 0-904387-57-7

Printed in Great Britain
by Redwood Burn Limited
Trowbridge & Esher

CONTENTS

CONTENTS

AUTHOR'S NOTE

I LOVE that typical Devon expression "A parcel of ol' crams," the delightfully non-committal phrase with which the native sums up and dismisses everything that he, and more particularly she, (*a*) cannot comprehend, (*b*) does not believe, (*c*) has no patience with, or (*d*) is entertained by but unwilling to praise. The nearest English equivalent I can think of is "A pack of nonsense," but it is an inadequate translation. "A parcel of ol' crams," like all the west-country idiom, is softer and less harsh to the ear than the more usual expression, but lacks none of its finality. It may be a simple commentary of merely personal reference, or it may be an invincible weapon capable of defeating the forces of science, learning and advancement, bringing professors, prime ministers, logicians, cranks, wits and 'ologians of every degree to a standstill as against a stone wall. You cannot argue past "A parcel of ol' crams." As a definition it is unarguable; it is the last word.

In illustration of its many and varied forms

of usefulness, here are a few instances I have met with.

MRS. A.: What did you think of the lecsher in the Ins'ichute last night, Mrs. B. about the calipsis of the mune, and the yarn about the earth gettin' in the light o' the zin and throwin' a shadow and makin' the mune go all black ?

MRS. B.: A parcel of ol' crams, Mrs. A.

MRS. A.: My opinion, zac'ly, Mrs. B.

. . . . .

FARMER: Some inspecter feller come out to my place tother day and said I was to have proper floors vor the cows in the shippens, with gutters so wide and so deep and winders such and such a heighth and watter laid on and I dunnaw what all. I told 'n 'twas a parcel of ol' crams.

. . . . .

A LANDLADY: I never come across such a party as I've got in now. They reckon they can't ait this and they can't ait that, they muzzen have buttcher's mait, only a lot of ol' green trade, and nothin' but brown braid, and no butter on their toast. What a parcel of 'ol crams!

. . . . .

A MOTHER: My Jimmy have come home with the tale that he've got to buy a tooth brish to take to skule and brish his teeth dree times a day, if ever you yeard such thing. I told 'n to tell the skule-maister 'twas a parcel of old crams.

. . . . .

A LABOURER: They parlyment fellers don't know no more than my ole wumman's cat. I went to a meetin' and yeard one of 'em praich up a long ol' rigmarole vor dree parts of a hour, and 'twas a parcel of ol' crams from start to finish.

. . . . .

MARRIED LADY: The men tries to make 'ee believe a parcel of ol' crams when they'm coortin' of 'ee, but 'tis a fresh lot altogether arter you'm married.

. . . . .

MRS. GOSSIP: Ol' Mother Tooze is everlastin' craikin' about her aches and pains, but I believe 'tis all a parcel of ol' crams, half aw't.

. . . . .

BILL BREWER: Did you go to the entertainment last night, Peter?

PETER DAVEY: Yaas. 'Twas very gude. There was a couple o' chaps from Exeter carried on with a parcel of ol' crams and purt' near made me bust me sides laafin.

. . . . .

OLD GEORGE: I ab'm got patience to harken to the ol' wireless. 'Tis nort but a parcel of ol' crams, all the lot aw't.

. . . . .

When my Muddlecombe neighbours see this book they will call it a "Parcel of ol' crams." So I have forestalled them.

A. J. COLES.

A PARCEL OF OL' CRAMS

I

THE NEW FIRE-ENGINE

I. AN OVERFLOW MEETING

If you'd bin along o' me when I looked in to the Rose an' Crown over to Barleycombe you'd 'a-said 'twas a minagerie and all the wild bastes had got into one cage, jidgin' by the racket that was gwain on inzide.

I had'n bin in the place fer weeks, and shude'n 'a-went in then, I don't suppose, only 'twas a very hot day, and I'd had a lot o' trapesin' about, and there was one or two I wanted to zee on business. I thought I shude likely to vind 'em in there and be able to talk things over quiet. But tell about one or two! I shude think there must 'a-bin half the men in the town there. And tell about quiet! They was all shoutin' one across tother like a mothers' meetin'. 'Twas like the crowd around a vootball match when the umpire-feller have gived a verdic' agin the local chaps. They was callin' and ray-callin' one-tother as if they'd bin a parcel of relations instead of jis' friends.

My dear days, what argifying there was gwain on to be sure. All I cude make out was, " No tid'n," " Yas 'tis," " You'm a liard," " You'm another," and all sitch like. 'Twas like hunderd rooks up in a tree.

I zee'd Varmer Jim Beer sot on a sate, so I squaised in bezide of he.

" What's up, maister ? " I says. " Is there another war on ? "

" They've jis' come from a council meetin', Jan," he saith, " and they've looked in yer to finish it off, zeem-zo."

" Council meetin'," I says. " Gude laur, I thought they'd ketched zomebody in the act of committin' mudder."

" You zee, Jan," says Varmer, " there's one or two mimbers o' the council yer, like Tommy Bamfield and Enry Brimmicombe and James Pearcey, and there's sevver'l more what have had to sit in the council-chimmer and harken to their speechifyin'. And of coorse, the spectators id'n allowed to say nothin' in there so they'm makin' up fer't now."

" I shude say they was, Mr. Beer. Zeemin' to me you'll require two or dree new mimbers fer the council by the time this lot have bin finished wai'. Looks like Nath Gudelan' will scat zomebody or else bust, purty zoon."

Nathaniel is a bit of a shoemaker, and if he was able to work half so vast as he'm able to tell he'd 'a-bin retired long ago.

"What's it all about?" I says. "Have the council proposed blawin' up the gas-works, or hangin' the way-warden or what?"

"'Tis this-yer new vire-ingine caper, Jan. Sivver'l mimbers o' the council have bin advocating fer ever so long to have a new moter vire-injine with works of his awn fer squirtin' watter, and this-aiv'min the majolity have voted fer it, so it have caused a middlin' gude rumpus, begad, amongs' they what was agin it. You wait till Nathaniel ketches sight o' you. He'll praich up the zame yarn all over again."

That very minute Nath looked over to where I was sot to, and he jumped up as if he'd bin shot. I might tell 'ee, Nath's a turrable chap fer usin' long words. Whether he knaws the meanin' of all aw'm or no I can't tell 'ee, but there's lots o' people what daun't.

"Hold thee baal!" he roared like a bull. "Now us'll be able to settle the matter. Bide quiet a minute, all of 'ee, and let me spaik. Darn' 'ee, I can't get a word in edge-ways."

They all bust out laafin' at that, cus o' coorse

Nath had done more tellin' than any two putt together.

"Yer's Jan Stewer o' Muddlecombe," he says. "Now us'll be able to get a unpartial opinion. Mr. Stewer's unresidential in the town and therefore he can give a verdic' without bigotiveness.

"Now then, Jan Stewer," he says, "you daun' reside to Barleycombe, and therefore Barleycombe rates daun' make no odds to you. And so I'm gwain to putt forth a plain, straightvorward question for your interpretation, on a very sayrious matter which is under discussion at the present moment, and I shall ax you to give a plain straightvorward answer; and this assemblance gathered herewith will undertake to abide by your verdic'. I shall nominate the question fair and square, wai'out any baitin' about the bush, and you mus' give your jidgment wai'out fear or favour. Now," he says, lookin' around the rume, "be I spaikin' with honesty and specification?"

"You'm spaikin' with a lot of unnecessary noise," says Tommy Bamfield. "Get on with the washin'."

"Well, now, Jan Stewer," says Nath, "I'll putt the whole matter to you clear and aboveboard, and let us yer your verdic', 'ees or no. Yer 'tis, then. Susposin' zomebody wanted to chuck away one thousand pound o' your own money down the drain, wude you agree to it?"

Aw, my dear zaul! What 'ullabaloo there was d'recly. Tell about givin' a verdic'. Lor, bless me, if I'd let off a gun nobody wude'n 'a-bin none the wiser. Everybody started holleyin' to-wance. Tommy jumped up, shoutin' to the top of his voice and wavin' his arms about; Enry Brimmacombe was knackin' on the table to help his words out; James Pearcey was jumpin' mad.

However, Tommy bein' a octioneer was able to overbaal the rest and get 'em middlin' quiet. And then he explained the matter as well as he cude with the others keepin' on cheemin' in. If they'd only kep' quiet and let one spaik to a time I shude have yer'd it all in half the time. But they cude'n hold their tongue ten words together.

"Now look-at-yer, Jan," says Mr. Bamfield, "I can give 'ee the whole rigmarole in one minute. You must understand, if there was a houze a-vire to-day in the borough of Barleycombe us cude'n putt 'n out."

"Rummage!" says Nath. "'Tid'n true."

"'Tis true," says Tommy, "and you can't deny it."

"Have'n us got a vire-brigade, then, and a vire-injine which cost a hunderd pound?"

"Yas, hunderd years agone. A blessid ole pump, got to be worked by hand, and can't squirt high nuff to watter a rose-bush. What about when Job Choak's work-shop ketched a-vire? The ole vire-injine wude'n pumpee far nuff to raiche the door, let alone up to the roof."

"And who's fault was that?" Nath holleyed. "Job shude have insured the place, same's I'd warned 'n scores o' times."

"And if he had of insured it, wude that make the watter squirt higher, mump'aid?" Tommy holleyed back at 'n. "Spausin' 'twas a dwellin' houze and there was li'l chillern asleep upstairs? Insurin' the houze wude'n save the chillern's lives, wude it?"

"Tis drowin' away the ratepayers' money," says Nath. "Thousand pound for a toy rattle-basket to rin about squirtin' watter. I reckon you ought to be made pay fer't out of yer awn pockets. Jis' cus 'tis other volks's money you daun' matter how you scats it abroad."

"Yer, yer," says Albert Venn. "Same's thik new-vangled watter-cart you spent all that money on. Who paid fer he? Us ratepayers. And what benevit do I get from 'en? I daun' want yer ole watter."

"You'd have more use fer'n if there was a drap o' gin in it, Albert," says Varmer Grant. Did'n 'um laaf; fer 'twas true as gospel.

"I tell 'ee what 'tis," says Nathaniel. "What with the new watter-carts and this-yer ole moter squirt, the council have got watter on the brain."

Everybody roared laafin'. But Tommy was upsides with 'n.

"No fear of gettin' watter 'pon thy brain, Nathaniel," he says, "cus there id'n rume fer't."

Everybody laafed again. I will say that for 'em; they did'n matter which zide they laafed at, so long as they injoyed a joke.

"'Twill be a waste o' gude money, same's tother was," says Albert. "You wad'n satisfied till you'd throwed away I dunnaw how much on a stoobid ole cockneyfied watter-cart. And what was the result? Us had no zooner got the blessid thing than it started to rain, and it rained every day fer two months on end, and spoiled the hay-harrest. A jidgment on the town I reckon that was. A jidgment on the town fer a wicked waste o' money. And you mark my words. 'Twill be the zame with this-yer ole moter vire-injine. I'll make a bet, after us gets 'en there waun't be a vire in the place."

"Let's hope and trist us waun't have no vire," says Tommy. "But 'tis the juty o' the council to be ready prepared in case us do. With the injine us have got now, if us had a proper bad vire you mid all-so-well have half-a-dizzen li'l boyes to spit to 'en. Be-as-'twill, us be gwain to have a new one, smack right up-to daate. And nex' Wainsdy wik there'll be a town's reception fer 'n, mayor and all. You'd better-way come over and witness it, Jan."

"If I can I will," I says.

"That's right," says Nathaniel. "And bring over a lighted cannle with 'ee, and let's zee if they can putt 'n out."

2. THE RECEPTION

Barleycombe volks had their reception o' the new moter vire-injine all right, and I shude'n think they'll virget it in a hurry. I shan't, anyway.

However, they zeemed very plaised with theirzels. James Pearcey went a couple o' mile out of his way the day following to call to my place and zee what I thought about it. Mrs. Endycott happened to be there callin' on my missis at the zame time, and I'm popped if James wad'n properly jumpin'.

"A eye-opener, wad'n it, Jan?" he says. "Don't you call 'twas a proper eye-opener? You did'n think a place the size o' Barleycombe cude accomplish such a sallybration, now did 'ee? Spaik yer mind. They cude'n 'a-done it more thereafter if it had bin Exeter or Plymouth, cude 'em ? "

" 'Twas well worth gwain to zee, James," I said.

" Worth gwain to zee! I shude think 'twas worth gwain to zee, if anybody had to go on their hands and knees. Never nothin' like it anywhere round thees parts. What I say now, is, 'tis a pity, 'pon me zaul, that a vire shude do any hurt, fer it do zeem a shame not to be able to use 'n a-plenty now us have got 'n. Not that I shude wish fer anybody's houze to ketch avire. But if such thing *was* to happen I'm bothered if us cude'n pumpee watter nuff to dout the vire and push the houze over if necessary."

" You want to get a vew new pipes fust, James," I says. " I vancy the ones you got now ban't hardly up to scratch."

" Aw, that wad'n nothin', maister. Us have got a-plenty new pipes belongin' to the injine, but they did'n care about unrollin' of 'em jis' fer that occasion, in case they wad'n able to roll 'em up again so nate as they was bevore. They thought 'twas better to use the old ones than to make the new ones untidy, and they wad'n hardly able to stand the pressure. That's all 'twas. They cude'n stand the pressure."

" I know that," I says. " If they *had* bin able to stand the pressure a bit better I shude'n have had so much cause to wish I'd took me umbrella."

" What, did 'um sprank the watter over 'ee, Mr. Stewer ? " says Mrs. Endycott.

" I dunnaw about sprank," I says. " I thought they'd took the bung out o' the watter-works fer a minute."

" There's one thing," says James, " the zin was so hot you cude'n hurt very much. But you missed the zight o' yer life, Mrs. Endycott. 'Twas a brave zight, wad'n it Jan, to zee thik butiful new injine, and the vire-brigade chaps sot up 'n top with their brassen helmets like gold itself, and their blue coats and shiny axes all complate. Tell the truth, Jan."

" 'Twas a brave show, sure nuff, James."

" I be dal'd if 'twad'n," he says. " And what volks there was there to zee it! I don't reckon there can be a turrable lot more to the Laurd Mayor's show up to Lunnon."

" What was there for 'em to zee ? " says mother. " What did 'ee do, all of 'ee ? "

" Us resayved the vire-injine, missis. And resayved 'n in a proper manner, too. You ax maister, there, if us did'n. He can testify whether us done it vitty or no."

" But what did 'ee want to resayve 'n vor ?

'Twas yer own property, wad'n it? I understood you'd a-bought 'n and paid fer 'n."

"That's right, missis. But you have to have a reception to do the thing proper. You know what a reception is, daun' 'ee?"

"I can't say I do, exac'ly. I've never zee'd a vire-injine close to. I've zee'd the one to Orcombe in the distance. But he did'n have no reception. They was forced to pull he along with hosses."

"You ab'm got the idaya, missis. A reception is a sarrymony. 'Tis what they calls a function. Do 'ee know what a function is?"

"No, ti-no. What do 'ee think, I've swallered a dictionary?"

"Well, to tell 'ee the truth," says James, "I did'n know what 'twas mezelf at the time. 'Twas the mayor what made use o' the word. When the majolity o' the council voted fer a new vire-injine the mayor said, 'Now us must have a function.'

"Up jumps Benjamin Tolley. Benjamin have bin the ringlaider of the contary party all the way through. Red-'ot agin the vire-injine he've a-bin, sure nuff.

"'That's right,' he says. 'Id'n that jis' what I prophesied? Wan expainse arter another. Fust us must have a new-vangled vire-injine. Slap he on the rates, says you. Then us got to build up a place to putt 'n into. Slap he on the rates. Now us have got to have a function to go along with 'n. Slap he on the rates! Nex' thing 'twill be us must have a place to keep the function in. Slap he on the rates likewise.'

"However, the mayor stood up and said he wude be to the expense o' the function out of his own pocket. 'And arter 'tis finished with I shall make 'n a present to Mr. Tolley,' he says, 'fer he to do what he mind to with 'n.'

"I cude zee by the way zome aw'm was laafin' that Benjamin had putt his voot in it and I be dalled if he had'n. A function is only zummin you have when you wants to make a show in public."

"Aw!" says Mrs. Endycott, "then it must 'a-bin a function that Lady Dumpsale was wearin' on her haid last Zindy. Supposed to be a hat, but if that wad'n a show in public I dunnaw what is."

"Never mind," says James. "Call it reception, or sarrymony, or function or whatever you will, nobody can't say but what us done the thing proper. Only to see what a host o' they newspaper chaps there was dappin' about, puttin' it all down in their li'l books, and every word that was said. And there 'twas nex' day, cullums aw't, fer the volks up in Lunnon to rade.

"And lots o' fellers there takin' likenesses. In fact, a chap had to keep his eyes open purty smart, else they'd take yer likeness when you wad'n lookin' yer best. Even as 'twas they ketched poor ole Benjamin Tolley jist as he was blawin' his nose, and so his faitures was all covered up with his pocket-ankcher. And the funny thing about ole Benjamin, although he was present to the reception agin the grain, pretendin', he was wild as a hawk when he zee'd his picsher on the paaper with no face.

"I noticed that with several aw'm," says James. "They cude'n say nothin' bad nuff about the ole injine bevore us had 'n, and done all they cude to frustrate 'n. But they was aiger nuff to be in the picsher, by jo. Laur bless 'ee, zoon's ever they zee'd the likeness-taker gettin' his ole machine ready, if they wad'n scammlin' up top o' the injine like so many monkeys to get the bes' position.

"And begad they wad'n missin' in the mayor's parler arterwards, when the aitin's and drinkin's was about. 'Twude make 'ee open yer eyes to zee zome aw'm lettin' back this-yer ole shampane trade. There's two or three aw'm won't think o' titchin' nothin' stronger than watter when they got to pay fer't theirzels, but if 'tis a sale or a rent-audit or anyplace where 'tis bein' gived away, they'll take whatever's gwain.

"There was ole Benjamin hiszelf, nosin' around to zee what there was free-gracious. So the mayor offered 'n a glass o' shampane.

"'Well, Mr. Councillor Tolley,' he says, 'I 'ope you'm gwain to drink health o' the new vire-injine.'

"'What ole trade do 'ee call this?' says Benjamin, lookin' in the glass and sniffin' to 'en.

"'That's a li'l drop o' function, Benjamin," says the mayor.

"Zo Benjamin he zoop to 'en once or twice, to try if 'twas fit to drink or no, and then he bide mapsin', like the ole wumman with the medicine to see whether 'tis the sort that do's her gude or no. And nex' minute he was gulgin' it like watter gwain down the sink. When 'twas all gone he screwed up his face and made a bivverin' noise as if it give 'n the creeps.

"'I can't think what people can zee in that nasty stuff,' he says.

"But 'twad'n many minutes bevore he inches close up to the mayor and says:

"'I beg pardon, Mr. Mayor, but I clane fergot to drink health to the vire-injine jis' now.

I 'ope you won't think 'twas done out o' contaryness. I wude'n like that to be thought fer one minute.'

" 'Better-way have a drop more function, councillor,' says the mayor. 'You mus' drink health to the vire-injine fer certin.'

" 'Wull, zooner than have it said I showed a wrong sperrit, yer worship. But only the laistest drop. Stop when I tells 'ee.'

" But Benjamin was so aiger to say 'Stop' that he cude'n get the word out quick nuff, and his glass was fulled right up to the brim. And he emp' 'n right down to the bottom.

" And vive minutes arterwards I yer'd 'n outzide tellin' away to the crowd nineteen to the dizzen, all about the wonderful new vire-injine; did'n they think he was a proper buty, and did'n they ought to be proud o' theirzel's to have sitch a vire-injine, and wad'n they lucky to have a council what was go-ahaid and up-to-daate and not stick-in-the-mud like zome plaaces? I tell 'ee, 'tis marvellous what a drop o' function can do."

" And is that all you done, Mr. Pearcey, drink shampane and have yer likeness took?"

" Lor bless 'ee, no, Mrs. Stewer. What about the precession, and the musickers and the spaiches. But Jan will tell 'ee all about that. I mus' be off. You never know; there might be a houze ketch avire bevore I gets back."

3. THE FIRST SQUIRT

There's no two ways about it, Barleycombe done the thing proper when they had the reception of their new moter vire-injine. I ab'm zee'd a precession to best that one not even on the Vith o' November. Ever so many o' the volks hanged out flags to their winders, and zome places they reached right across the strate. There to Westgate they putt up a lovely gurt arch, all covered in evergreens and ribbins and mottoes. I shude think it must have purt' near broke their hearts to take 'n down again.

The Barleycombe Town Band walked to the haid o' the precession; and I shude say if the amount o' weend they chaps blawed into their musics cude 'a-bin putt inzide the vire-injine 'twude 'a-squirted the watter right up over the church tower. How they cude keep on like it with such blazin' hot zin I can't think. Speshly Bill Way lettin' into the big drum. I'm popped if he wad'n rinnin' down into straimes of swattin'. Half-ways up the strate Bill tooked off his coat and let the triangle chap have it to carr'. Then come the policemen two be two, like a ridgment o' sawjers if there'd only bin a few more of 'em. And behind they again come Wi'yum Crossland what alwis walks bevore the mayor. Dressed up like the lord high cockolorum Wi'yum was, carr'in' a long stick with a gurt gold knob pon-tap, and his nose sticked up in the air like's-if he'd got the King of England behind 'n. Do's it vine, Wi'yum do, and staps out that stiff, you'd think he had'n got a joint in his body.

And then come the mayor hiszelf, in his vine urd coat with the rabbit skeen around the top and bottom, and his cocked 'at pokin' out bevore and behind, and a butiful golden chain around his neck, lookin' like's if he'd winned the fus' prize and champion to the agricultural show.

Nex' come the mimbers o' the council. They was all in the precession, bless yer 'art, whe'er they'd voted fer the vire-injine or no. You wude 'a-thought they what fought agin it all the way droo the piece wude bide away from the precession and rayfuse to have aught to do wai't. But I'd defy anybody to tell which was which, cus they was blowin' out their chests as much as the rest. Most aw'm had got on long-tail coats and long-sleeve hats, and looked up turrable smart, begad. Speshly they what had got on their own hats. Thomas Bidgude was wearin' the box-hat his vather left 'en. But Thomas id'n the man his father was and his haid wude'n come to it, so he was forced to putt a strip o' paaper all around the inzide of his hat. 'Twude 'a-bin all right if one end o' the paaper had'n sticked out behind like a pig-tail. And o' coorse Tom was the only body what cude'n zee it.

Then come all the clubs with their banners, and their li'l apperns, and their tettivations around their necks, and Colonel Brown with all the sawjers he cude hatch up. Then there was a parcel o' maidens all dressed up in white gowns carr'ing bunches o' flowers. Very purty they did look; and then come the Guild to give the ole maids a chance.

And there was heaps more bezides, passens and docters and ambalance and the chaps what works for the council and the officials as well.

But the thing what tooked everybody's eye was the vire-injine hiszelf. He did look grand and no mistaake, rid as vire and shinin' like a new zixpence, with the brass aw 'n like gold, and the vire-brigade chaps sot up 'n top with their gurt hats all of a glitter and their blue coats and shiny buttons. 'Twas a brave zight, begad, and no wonder the volks did cheer when he went past.

And never a hoss in the sharps, but gwain along by hiszelf so aisy and suant, with Urchet Passmore dinging the bell all the way jis' like rale.

When the precession come to the Square the vire-injine stapped right bevore the Guil'all, and the volks stood all out around where they cude view what was gwain on. The mayor stood up top the injine and made a vine spaich. At laiste, I shude imagine 'twas a vine spaich by the way he worked his arms about and his jaws went up and down. But his voice id'n the loudest in the world, and from where us stood us cude'n ketch a word. However, by watchin' they what was a bit handier to 'en us cude tell when to clap and when to laaf and when to say "Yer, yer," and so forth. So us managed purty well.

When the mayor had vinished yappin' and us had give 'n a gude clap, the mayoress got up to name the vire-injine. Us cude'n ketch what her said, but I shude think her made a very gude spaich, and then her had a bottle and give 'n a scat up agin the injine and spranked the stuff all about the place and then her named the injine. "Lady May" her was called, arter Zur Thomas Bowden's wive. But Joe Lane called 'n "Scarlet Rinner," and that's the name he've gone by ever since.

Ned Passcoe was stood next to me. "What was inzide o' thikky bottle do you reckon, maister?" he said.

"Wine, I reckon, Ned."

"Aw, dear, dear, what a pity, to think o' wastin' gude stuff like that. I cude 'a-putt it to a better purpose I know, a hot day like this."

Then the policeman come and made us all stand further back out the way, cus the injine was gwain to pumpee. But everybody was excited to zee what was gwain to happen, so they graj'ly got vore again, through everybody tryin' to be in front.

Mr. Robert Cumes is the boss o' the vire-brigade, and when he blowed his wissel all the chaps flipped off the injine, and started rishin' around like a parcel o' rabbuts. They joined up all the pipes and putt one end into the watter and screwed the nozzle on tother end. Edwert Tozer is what you might term the foreman nozzle-holder, and he prides hiszelf on the way he do's it. He've winned sivver'l prizes in competition, Edwert have, fer nozzle-holdin', and beat chaps from up the country. He can aim thik strame o' watter as straight as zome men cude aim a gun. Everybody was aiger to zee Edwert prevorm with a new injine behine 'en, and 'twas knowed all over the town that he ordained making the weathercock on the Guil'all spin around like a top. There was a-plenty prepared to bet a shullin that he'd do it, too.

Bevore you cude say " knive " everything was ready, and all attention was on Edwert. And I must say, he looked very well stood all by hiszelf in the middle o' the ring with his smart new clothes and his brassen hat and the nozzle pointing up in the air. Us was all holding our breath, with one eye on the ole weathercock.

Unforchnitly, Edwert had no idaya of the strength of a moter injine. He'd alwis bin accustomed to the chaps pumpin' by hand, and then he cude hold the nozzle aisy. But when Cap'm Cumes give the word and the injine beginned to let rip—aw, my dear zaul! How can I discribe what happened! No words cude do it.

Fer one thing, the chap what turned on the watter shude 'a-done it a bit to a time, but he stoobidly let it go full butt. The nozzle gived a kick like a mule and knacked poor Edwert back'erds, tap-over-tail, jis' like Ole Aunt Sally. He done his best to hang on to 'en, but he might as well try to hold a train. The ole nozzle flied out of his hands like a rocket and then lied down in the rawd and wriggled about jis' like some enormous gurt feesh took out o' the watter, and sent a watter-spout in all derections. The fust strame ketched the mayor and corporation as clane as a wissle, and there was box 'ats flyin' about like leaves in October. Edwert Tozer made a jump at the nozzle to try to control 'n, but the ole nozzle turned on 'en and the nex' thing us zee'd was Edwert's butiful new brassen hat up top o' the lamp-paust and Edwert hiszelf swimmin' about in the road graspin' fer breath.

Half a dizzen o' the vire-brigade chaps tried to turn off the watter, but they was so excited they got in one-tother's way and 'twas a minute or two bevore they cude stop it from spurtin'. And what the ole nozzle done in that time you'd hardly believe. Anybody wude think he had eyes to zee. He went all around the crowd and shared out the watt r between 'em so's nobody shude be jellis, and last of all he lied still and poured a strame in amongs' the women's guild.

Ole Ned Passcoe was dancin' fer joy. His missis is one o' the guild and her's fer everlastin' naggin' at Ned becus he daun't drink watter instead o' so much geen.

" Now they'm 'appy," says Ned. " Now they must be 'appy fer certin. They'm alwis zingin' ' Watter fer me, watter fer me,' and I'm jiggered if they have'n got their wish. They'm gettin' all the watter they wants."

However, I was very lucky. The ole nozzle did'n hap'm to zee me, so I was able to laaf at the rest. They stopped the rush of watter to-last, and then they putt two chaps on the nozzle so's to hold 'n back. And this time they let the watter in a bit more aisy, and when 'twas full on I'm beggered if it wad'n a wonderful sight. The watter spurted right up over the Guil'all without titchin'. Matter o' fact, although they wad'n aware aw't at the time, 'twas pourin' strames down the people's chimleys at the back, and it cost the council hunderds o' pounds arterwards in damages. But us did'n knaw that, and the volks cheered like mad to zee the watter squirtin' up so high. Even they what had had a zoakin' clapped their hands and cheered.

But as I said bevore, they ole pipes wude'n stand the strain, and jist as I was gwain to cheer along o' the rest wan of 'em busted all of a sudden right where I was stood to. I'd almost got me voot on the place, so you can imagine how it sarved me. All up my trouser-ligs, up me sleeves, inzide and outzide alike. Bevore I'd got time to move I was wet right in droo to the skeen. If I'd jumped in the say with me clothes on I cude'n 'a-bin no wetter. And all they miles to go.

"Thank 'ee, very much," I said. "I'm gwain 'ome. You can keep yer ole vire-injine. His looks is all right, but I don't like his manners."

II

SALE NOW ON

I'VE yeard it said bevore now that if you was to have a wild baiste, like a lyon or a taygur, when 'twas a baby and rare it up fer a pet he'd be all right till he tasted blid, and then there'd be no holdin' aw'n. You might larn 'en to be as gentle as a kitten and volley about like a dog, or lay down till you says " policeman," or sit up and beg, or balance a biscuit on his nose, or do any mortle thing so-long as he don't taste blid. But the minute he've tasted blid he goes back to his wild nature d'recly, and he'll spring upon 'ee, and tear 'ee all abroad and ait 'ee up as soon as look, although you might be the bes' friend he ever had and as gude as a mother to 'en.

That's what I've bin told by volks what has read it in bukes, but whe'er 'tis true or no I can't zay, cus I never keeped a lyon ner a taygur and don't intend to.

But I fancy the women-volk is zummin the zame in a manner o' spaikin'. Now, I don't want fer you to misjidge my mainin'. I ban't tryin' to liken the women-volk to wild animals. All as I mean is, there's certin things will make a wumman alter her nature fer the time, and get up to all manner of capers which any other time her wude'n draime about.

And the most thing I know to sarve a wumman like that is a " Zale." You mention a shop to a wumman where they'm " zellin' off" and her'll be about as contented and paiceful as a long-dog on a chain that have just zee'd a rabbut bolt. A zale is the zame to a meek and gentle wumman as blid is to a tame taygur.

And I ban't tellin' about zummat I've read in a buke this time. 'Tis my own experience, which I've bin droo now lately.

Me and mother went down to Plymouth to stap a day or two along o' James Quant and his wive, Lucy. And mother's attack started comin' on bevore us had been in the place ten minutes.

James and Lucy come to the station to meet us, and us went back on one o' they yaller buses. All the way through the strate they two women was jiggin' about like jack-in-the-boxes, fust one zide and then t'other.

" There's a zale on there," Lucy Quant wude go, pointin' to a shop, and mother wude dap around as if a appledrain had stinged her on the neck or zomewhere. " They got zome wonderful bargins there in the shape o' gloves, and stockin's is marked down half-price."

" You don't say so," says Ann. " I ab'm had a new pair o' gloves I dunnaw when, and as fer stockin's—I've mended all mine till there's more darn than aught else. I mus' look in there fust opportunity."

" Ees, and there's another place you ought to go to bevore 'tis too late. They've got a genuine zale on. Lovely hats, properly givin' away."

" That's the very thing I wants, is a new hat. I'm ashamed to be zee'd in the one I've got now."

" Well, that's the place for 'ee then. But if you wants any woolly things, yer's a shop where they'm zellin' off, lookee, and the things is marked redicklus prices. I'm sure you cude zave yer railway fare in there. And as fer jumpers, they've got hunderds, all shapes and sizes, and ready to take almost anythin' you mind to offer fer 'em."

" What do 'em mean by jumpers, James ? " I says.

" Cude'n tell 'ee, Jan. The only jumpers I knows aught about is what us tries to get rids of by every means in our power. If there's one in the houze which us might have picked up to the pichsers or zome place else, mother can't rest till he'm ketched. And now they'm tellin' about payin' money fer 'em! "

"That's stoobid," I says. "Us can get all us wants o' they fer nothin'."

"There's no notice to be took o' the women-volk just about now, Jan," he says. "They goes partially mazed when the zales is on. I've yer'd nothin' else in my houze fer the past week but ribbins and remnants, velveteen and scrape-de-sheen, long skirts and short skirts, five and 'leb'm-three, trimmed and untrimmed, overalls and underalls, and heaps o' things that people once upon a time didn' hardly like to hang out on the line, never mind talk about."

"Shut up, yer gurt gawk," says Mrs. Quant. "You don't understand nothin' about it."

But I'm beggered if James wad'n right. When my missis and his missis and their two maidens got together 'twas nothin' else but the ole zales. Fust one wude dap up over stairs and take down a parcel o' things her'd purchased, and then another wude display zome garment which her'd had fer half price. And so her ought to, fer it wad'n more 'n half the size they used to be. And every fresh thing her zee'd my Ann wude declare was exac'ly what her was wantin'.

Nex' mornin' mother was up soon's ever 'twas dayslight, cus James's wive said 'twas advisable to get to the shops early bevore there was many other women about. Lucy cude'n go out herzelf not till later in the day, so mother said I must go along with her cus very likely us might zee zummat gwain cheap that wude do fer me.

My gudeness gracious, what a vield day us had trapesing around to they ole shops. How any wumman cude indure it I can't think. I was dog-tired, zick and weary bevore 'twas half over, but mother kep' gwain like a two-year-old. Wherever her glimpsed the word " Zale " on a winder her was off like a tarrier arter a rat. Her'd flip across the strate right in front o' the moters and make my 'art come up in me mouthe. But her cude'n zee no danger. All her cude zee was " Zale Now On," and her was feared of her life zome other wumman wude get in fust and pick up all the bargins.

And the way her did drag me back and vore and round and round in they ole shops was zummin shameful. If that's what they call not very many about, I'm bothered if I shude care to be there when the place is full up. I never was in among so many women in me life bevore. And there wad'n manners nuff 'mongst the whole lot aw'm to cover up a dripmy-bit. They was pushin' and shovin' and pullin' the things about. 'Pon me zaul, I almost thought they'd come to vightin' zometimes. I tried ever so many times to flip outzide, but mother took gude care I did'n escape. When her zee'd me inchin' off her'd dray my attention to zummin.

" Look, father, look to this. Only vower an' leb'mpence dree-vardens. Daun' you call that's cheap? " And then her'd hold up zome redecklus garment that I wude'n knaw the name of, and shude'n be expected to, nuther. Made me veel that nervous and uncomferable, I did'n hardly know which way to look, zometimes. Then her'd ketch zight of a heap o' things some other part o' the shop, and away-to-go, like a cat arter a mouze, hoikin' me along too. Then her'd come across a lot of hats, and putt one on her haid and ax me what her looked like. And when I told her her only got annoyed.

But I was forced to laaf zometimes at the things mother wude say to they shop-maidens. What a different tale her told bevore their face and behind their back.

" Look, father," her'd say to me when nobody else was about, " only nine and leb'm-three. (Everything was zummin and leb'm-three. I spause if 'twas tain shullins 'twude be dear; but nine and leb'm-three is cheap.) That's no money 't all for it, is it? " her'd zay. " If I was to buy that to Thorne's to Barleycombe 'twude be vifteen shullins, every penny aw't."

Then up wude come one o' the maidens and ax mother if her wanted to buy it.

" Not at that price, my dear. I thought you was spaused to be zellin' off. Why, I cude get it less than that home. If you was to take off a shullin it might be worth considerin'."

And zometimes they'd knock back a shullin, or praps they'd only knock back zixpence. But if 'twas only a penny Ann wude be so-proud as a paycock. Her bought sevver'l things her did'n want one bit in the world, zimply 'cus her bate back the price. I know her did.

And every time her purchased aught her let me have it to carr', so that did'n make it no more aisy fer me to shove me way droo they crowds o' women-volk, you mid be sure. And they did'n make way fer me, nuther. They was all too aiger fer their bargins to consider me. But mother wude get wild as a hawk if I wad'n zac'ly where her expected to vind me.

"Why don't you go where I go?" her says.

"Bless the wumman," I says, "I can't go where I like. I've got to go where I'm pushed."

And the funny part aw' 't was, every time us got out in the strate from one o' they shops, mother wude say, "My gudeness, how the time do fly. We mus' be gettin' back."

I would be glad as a burd, and I'd say, "Ees, they'll think us be lost."

So us wude go on about a gun-shot, and I wude do my best to keep mother's attention on zummin straight a-haid; but 'twas no gude.

All of a sudden her'd stap short like a hoss refusin' a jump.

"Ullaw! They've got a zale on over there, lookee. Us'll jis' flip across and zee what they've got in the winder. 'Twon't take a minute. Us need'n go inzide 'cus I know there's nothin' there I wants."

'Twas no gude me sayin' aught. Well, I cude'n very well, 'cus by this time her was half-ways across the strate, so the only thing fer me was to volley on behind. And then 'twude be the zame ole rigmarole over again.

"I don't call this very much of a zale. Everything's dear, I reckon. Jis' look at thik hat fer eight-an'-leb'm. Redecklus, I call it. They anbrellas ban't very bad value fer vive-an'-leb'm. I cude do with a new anbrella, but I dersay all the best aw'm be picked out by now. That's cheap ribbin at vi'pence-dree-vardens. Jane cude 'a-done with a vew yards o' that, I'll warrant, and 'twude be a shullin' a yard into Barleycombe. But all the best colours is gone, I'll bet a guinea. Zome volks is that selfish, they'd buy a thing they didn't want sooner than let another body have it. Well, I don't zee nothin' yer worth havin'. I don't think very much o' this shop, I must say. I dersay they've got all their best bargins inside. Us'll jis' pop in and look around a minute. Us won't stop, 'cus I don't want to buy nothin'. Don't talk so stoobid. Of *coorse* you can come een. You won't look half so fulish stood inzide the door as you will stuck out there in the strate with all they parcels. And 'tid'n as though I was gwain to stap any time."

So there I was in the zame quandairy all over again.

Ees, and when us got back to the houze, what do you think? Lucy Quant axed my wive whether her'd done any shoppin' or no.

"Nothin' to spaik of," her saith. "Us went in one or two shops, but I cude'n inspec' the things properly 'cus my ole man was such a fidget, keepin' on all the time. But I shall go and have another look around when I've had a bit of a rest."

"Aw, will 'ee?" I says to mezelf. "Then Jan's gwain to be lost, and nobody won't be able to vind 'en till 'tis too late."

III

SPEECH ON A CHURCH CLOCK

YOU can talk about yer wonderful spaich-makers in the Houze o' Parlyment, or paasens in the pole-pit, or the cheapjack to Barleycombe Vair, but I reckon Jim Wonnacott cude bate the lot o' min. For makin' a peeration out o' nothing, and praichin' up a long ole yarn without anybody being any the wiser I never come across the aiqual of 'n. With such a gift as he've got, if he only'd had a bit more eddication he might 'a-bin a prime minister, or a gurt lawyer gettin' his thousands a year; instead of a sort of a parish factotum, gettin' a job yer and there wherever 'tis aisiest.

See what a spaich he made to the meetin' up to the skulerume when 'twas proposed to collect a lot o' money and erect a village clock in the church tower. Squire interduced the subjic' as the sayin' is, and said 'twas a thing that was wanted very bad.

"There id'n a clock in the place that anybody can swear by," says the Squire. "Very often there's two or dree differnt times in the village, and one says 'tis one thing and one says 'tis another thing, and that causes a lot o' fuss and bother. But if us had a clock in the church tower everybody cude go by it, and 'twude be very convaynient fer people gwain to church, or the chillern gwain to skule, and chaps to lef' work by," and so on and so forth.

So then he axed all they what had any views on the matter to putt 'em forth. And zome was for it and zome was agin' it; and they sot in their sates and spoked a vew words. And zome did'n knaw which way they was, and they mostly stood up and said a doost of a lot.

But Jim Wonnacott got up on his hine ligs and made a spaich.

"Wull, yer honour," he says, "you've axed us to say what us thinks about the matter so I'll tell 'ee what I thinks. And I be gwain to tell 'ee straight, wai'out any hummin' and ha-in'; and they what daun' like it mus' do tother thing. My moral alwis is, when you've got aught to say, say it, and never mind about nobody. I ban't one o' they what keeps their principles up their sleeve. Honesty's the best policy, is my motive, and I never turns from it without there's a raison fer't. So I'll tell ee' what I thinks of this-yer clock consarn, and that is, I'm darned if I knaws what to think. There you be. That's spaikin' straight out, without any baitin' about the bush. I've thought about it, and I've turned it auver in me mind, and that's my candid opinion. I dunnaw what to think about it, and I'd defy anybody to knaw what to think about it. Of coorse, you can say this, that and tother thing about it, and 'tis so-an-so and sitch like. But when you comes to weigh it all up, can you be sure about it? Of coorse you can't, and 'tis no gude to say otherwise. I believes in lookin' at things in advance; not go rinnin' yer haid up agin' a wall and then vind yerzelf in a hole.

"You say, 'Have a clock in the church tower.' All well and gude. But what about when you've got 'n there? You might say clocks is clocks; and so they be to a certain extaint. Us knows they ban't weel-barras ner yet drashin'-machines. But there's a lot o' differnce in clocks, as you do know so-well as I can tell 'ee. Some is too slow and some is too vast. But what us wants is one that's zac'ly in the middle, neether one thing ner tother. Or if there's any differnce at all he shude be a bit on the vore zide, so if you arrived to a place a trifle laate you'd be zac'ly to time.

"Us have got a clock home, which us have had ever since I was a li'l tacker. My vather had 'n of poor ole Varmer Balls to Zilworthy the night bevore he was sold up. I can remember 'em takin' the clock home inzide the hoss's veed-bag, cus, o' cou'se, everything was supposed to be in the zale. But Varmer reckoned my vather had bin very gude to 'en, and he wished fer 'n to make zummin out aw't and so he let 'n have the clock. And a very gude clock he is, too, if you keep zummin about the thickness of yer hand in under one leg, cus he loppeth auver a bit to one zide.

"But he'll never make 'ee laate, cus he alwis travels on a-haid, so us have never missed the train by 'en, yet. Matter o' fact, more 'n once us have ketched a train earlier than the one us intended. The only trouble is when he gets more 'n half a day vast you've got to remember that's to-morra's time and not to-day's, else you might think he was behind. And, o' cou'se, us can alwis shift the hands a bit when they gets out of all correspondence.

"'But when you tells about stickin' a clock up in church tower, that's another matter altogether. I know it is done. And I can't zay as I've never zee'd such thing, becus I have. I've zee'd it auver to Li'l Raxun. They've got a clock poked up in church tower, same's you say. But after that, no notice is to be took of the Raxun volks. They'm a lurripin', scammle-vooted lot, what never knows where they'm gwain till they gets there, and then they'm surprised to vind where they'm to; beggin' Zam Higgs's pardon, as I zee he's auver yer from Raxun. Not that he's very much better than the rest, after that.

"As I zay, they've got a clock to Raxun, and I daun' suppose anybody ever looks at 'n. Or if they do a vat lot o' gude it do's 'em. Look at their crops. Furthest behind of any parish fer miles around. I reckon their clock mus' be about a vortnight slow.

"What I sez about a clock in church tower is this. You putt'th 'en there, and there 'tis; and there it have got to bide. You can't take 'n about with 'ee, and no matter what part o' the parish you be to, if you wants to know the time you got to trapes all the way to the church to vind out. Susposin' I be workin' to Ruddiver Bottom and I wants to know if 'tis time to lef' work. I've got to tramp all up droo Aish and Pitt right into the village. Wull, and by the time I got back to Ruddiver Bottom I shude want to know the time again. So I shude have that journey auver again. I shude spend half the day walkin' up to zee the clock, and tother half walkin' back. So a fat lot o' work I shude do, shude'n I?

"Of coorse, you zay, 'Make 'n to strike the howers, so a feller can yer the time wai'out gwain to look.' That's all right, and I shude be the last to say aught agin it. But I daun' zee that I shude be a lot better off than I was bevore.

" Susposin', as I said jis' now, I was to work to Ruddiver and I wanted to know what time 'twas. I've got to stand there doin' nort, ab'm I, waitin' fer the clock to strike. Fer certin I have ; cus if I was to go kickin' up a clatter with me hook or shovel or whatever tool I was usin' I shude never yer a zound all down there. Of coorse, I knows I need'n stand. I cude sit in under the hedge. But that don't get the work done, do it ? And it don't make the clock strike no quicker. And furthermore, susposin' when I stapped to harken it was only two minutes gone the hower. I've got to wait eight an' vifty minutes bevore I shall know the time. And even then, all that distance away and if the weend shude happen to be contry, I cude'n be sure if I'd counted the strokes right. I shude'n knaw fer certin whe'er 'twas 'leb'm or twelve. I shude be in two minds about it. And what wude be the consequence ? I shude have all that journey up the hill to glimpse the clock.

" Whereas, if there had'n bin no clock at all, what shude I have said to mezelf ? I shude have said, ' Jim Wonnacott, what time is it dost think ? ' And then I shude have answered to mezelf, ' Wull, yer tongue is claivin' unto the roof o' yer mouthe and yer stommick's most mortle leery. It mus' be dinner-time.' And that wude be the end aw't. But then, o' cou'se, a body id'n alwis workin' to Ruddiver Bottom, and therefore it wude'n apply in every case. A chap workin' anywhere the higher zide o' the village wude'n have no excuse fer knackin' off bevore the time; so I won't say but what this-yer clock might do gude as well as harm."

"Well, Wonnacott," says the Squire, "us have yer'd what you have to say, and now will 'ee tell us whe'er you'm in favour o' the clock or no?"

"Jist exac'ly what I've said, yer honour. I've spoked out my mind, and now 'tis fer every other body to do the zame. What I means I says, and what I says I means, and I daun' care fer the next. You've had my opinion and you'm welcome to it. But nobody can't say but what I've spoked out plain and honest."

IV

TOM TOLLEY'S BAND

I. HOW IT WAS STARTED

"ULLAW! Yer's Mr. George Elworthy, I zee. Be you gwain to ride in along o' we, Mr. Elworthy?"

"Yas, Mrs. Snell, if you'll have me."

"Sit down yer, where I can talk to 'ee. 'Tis gude to zee a strange face, even if 'tid'n very much of a one to look at. What's the latest out your way, then?"

"Can't tell 'ee, hardly, missis. It have'n happened yet."

"What have'n happened?"

"Why, the latest."

"Aw, git-'long! There's usu'ly zummin gwain on in your parish."

"Aw, ees. There's usu'ly zummin gwain on. Or if 'tid'n that 'tis zummin else. You knows us have got a band started, fer certin?"

"Band, Mr. Elworthy? What do 'ee mean, band?"

"Well, I spause you knows what a band is, daun' 'ee? You will when you yers this wan, anyway."

"Do you mean music, George?" says Ned Annaferd.

"I wude'n hardly go so fur as that, Ned. I wude'n go so fur as to term it music. But 'tis a noise, anyway. And 'tis a noise which they makes a-purpose. They reckons 'tis gwain to turn into music wan o' these days. I have'n noticed much prospec' o' the change coming, not yet, but us can only hope fer the best."

"What be 'ee gettin' now, then, George; the worst?"

"I hope so, Ned. I hope so, with all me 'art and zaul. For if it gets any worse than 'tis now 'twill be a bad job, begad."

"I never zee'd sitch a lot as the volks in Week parish," says Mrs. Snell. "You'm alwis up to zome fresh caper. You don't zeem to be able to rest, zome'ow."

"No, and neether wude'n you be able to rest, missis, if you was livin' anywhere in the parish at the present time. Not while there's band-practising gwain on, anyway."

"But they ban't practising all the time, I don't suppause."

"No, I don't suppause they be, reely. It only zeems like it. Twice a week they ordains having what they terms the band practice. But laur bless yer 'art, it don't finish with that. That's only when they meets to wan place and do's their blawin' all together. But in between times they goes tryin' it over in their own houses whenever they gets a minute to spare. So if one id'n kickin' up a din another is.

"When Sid Burridge's euphonian id'n moanin' up to the blacksmith's shop, Bill Bennett's trambone is groanin' down to the raiding-rume. Bill's the caretaker to the raiding-rume, and he cude'n have no better way of caretakin' than what that is. No fear of anybody comin' in and biss'ling up the place while he'm gettin' that howlin', growlin' noise off his chest; cus if you wants to rade what's on the papers you've got to say it out loud else you can't yer what you'm thinkin' about.

"If you goes into the post-orfice to buy a stamp you must bide and wait till James Widmore comes to the end o' the chune with his ole cornet. If you happens to go in jis when he've started the second verse 'tis a buster, 'cus he will persist in playin' the choriss over twice.

"You can't look into the Rid Lion fer a drink wai-out havin' to tell Zam Blackler, the lan'lord, what you thinks o' 'this-yer li'l zolo on his clar'net,' which he'll sit up tap the barreel and play to 'ee when you wants to injoy yer beer.

And the worst aw't is, you dursen tell 'n the truth, 'cus Zammy's a gurt big chap with a nasty temper."

" 'Twill be all right arter a bit, I dersay," says Tom Zalter, " when they gets a bit more used to it."

" So they keeps tellin' me," says George, shaking his haid. " But how long 'twill take to get used to it I wude'n like to say. I'm feared 'twill be zummin' like the feller what larned his pig the way to live wai'out aiting. Jist as he'd got used to it the blessid pig took and daied. The worst thing I zees about it, 'tis ap' to get the village a bad name."

" How do 'ee make that out ? "

" Well, fer certin, strangers passin' droo the strate in their moters must imagine 'tis eetherways zomebody turrable zick and bad, or else 'tis the day fer killin' pigs. So they don't stap and look around and spend money in the place, but goes on to the nex' village."

" What's their idaya in havin' a band, George ? Jis' fer their awn pleasure, I suppause ? "

" It can't be fer no other body's, Tom, that's a certin sure thing. But they'm gwain to do wonders, bless yer 'art. Gwain to make no end o' money, they be, when they've larned the way to play chunes."

" How can 'um do that ? " says Mrs. Snell.

" Why, they reckons they'm gwain to get ingagements to go about to sports and feets, and play to concerts, and all sitch-like, and get paid money fer't. I hope my haid won't ache bevore it comes true."

" I did'n know," says Ned, " whether they ordained gwain in fer they band-contests or no. I zee'd on the paper that zome Cornwall chaps winned the fust prize up to Lunnon, tother day."

" I know all about that," says George. " But our band is gwain to whack they all to nothing nex' year, by all accounts. They'm telling about gwain up to the Cristial Palace to play agin the bands from all over the country. But I tells 'em they don't need to go to that expense, cus if they continues increasin' the way they'm gwain on now they'll be able to bide home and play, and the jidges will be able to yer 'em up to the Cristial Palace jis' as aisy as the chaps out to Pottery can yer the ' lef'-work ' whistle."

" Ban't you wan o' the band then, Mr. Elworthy ? "

" Not now, Mrs. Snell. I did join in fust-along, cus I thought praps I shude be able to suffer it better if I was taking part, and assisting to make some o' the noise. But my bellises wad'n powerful nuff to blow wan o' they brassen musics to the extent they wanted it done. So they let me have a go to the triangle, 'cus he did'n require no weend. They hanged he up to me left thumb with a bit o' cord and let me have a li'l bar of ire about a voot long to strike 'n with me right hand. But every time I went to give the ole triangle a extry gude scat I fetched me thumb a whack instaid. And you zee, Tom Tolley, the bandmaster, is a part of a methody parsen and he said he wad'n gwain to have sitch language used in his band. So I said I wad'n gwain to have my thumb used fer anvil, and I thought I'd better-way give up tryin' to be a musicker."

"What about the big drum, George?" says Tom. "I shude a-thought he wude have suited 'ee, cus it don't take very much weend to play that one fer certin."

"I thought about the big drum, Tom," says George. "But he belongs to Peter Sillage, so therefore nobody but Peter must be allowed to play 'en. That's where the trouble's to. Everybody what have got a instrument of his own expects to be the one to play 'en, never mind whether he've got any eye fer music or no."

"I spause they wude'n have the instruments if they cude'n play 'em," says Mrs. Snell.

"That don't signify, missis," says George.

"You've got a butiful pair of yeomanry-calvary trousers home, with yaller trimmin's all down both zides. I know you have, cus you've showed 'em to me bevore now. But becus you've got 'em that don't mean to say you can wear 'em. At laiste I never——"

"Hold thee baal, thee gurt gawk," says missis. "They belonged to my gran'fer, did'n 'em?"

"Well, and 'tis the zame by they musics. They've come down like the sins o' the vathers to the third and vorth ginerations. Only they'm visited on the neighbours instead of on the chillern. Most o' they musics belonged to the vathers and gran'vathers o' the chaps what have got 'em now. So 'tid'n to say they can play 'em becus they've got 'em, any more than Mrs. Snell cude wear——"

"That's quite sufficient, George Elworthy," says missis. "Us be talkin' about your band, not my gran'fer's univorm."

"'Tis quite right what you say, George," says Tom Zalter. "I can mind as well as anything when Sarjin-Major Triscott use to ride his hoss with they vine togs on; and that's gwain back a vew years, 'cus I wad'n but a li'l tacker at the time. And turrable smart he looked too, I be dal'd if he did'n; and the whole parish use to stap work to view 'n when he did ride off to the manoovers. But he were a tall, thinnish man, so fer certin Mrs. Snell cude'n——"

"Tom Zalter, if thee dissen bide quiet I'll give thee a scat with my anbrella, I will. Now, Mr. Elworthy, be you gwain to talk sainse or no?"

"Yas, missis, I was gwain to tell 'ee how the band come to be fust insigated; and that was through the means of Zammy Blackler fishin' out the ole clar'net which belonged to his gran'vather, daid an' gone this vorty year."

"Did'n he know he had 'n, then?"

"He did and he did'n, if you understand. Matter o' fac', the ole clar'net had been tooked apart zome time or 'nother and Mrs. Blackler was usin' the thick end fer a cannlestick. Made a hanzum cannlestick he did, and stood up butiful.

"Well, and wan day Tom Tolley hap'm to zee Mrs. Blackler carr'ing this-yer cannlestick, with a lighted cannle in 'en. You know Tom Tolley o' cou'se? A proper musicker Tom is, and plays the orgin to the chapel.

"'Whatever have you got there, Mrs. Blackler?' he says.

"'Where, Mr. Tolley?'

"'Don't you know that's wan end of a clar'net?'

"'No, I did'n know what 'twas. He makes a rare cannlestick, I know that.'

"So then Tom explained 'twas half a music and there shude be another piece like it. Zammy Blackler happened to come in the rume at the zame time, and yer'd what he said.

"'I'm beggered if you ban't right, Tommy,' he says. 'He belonged to my ole gran'fer, and now you come to mention it he use to be double the length and had sevver'l more holes.'

"Well, and then Mrs. Blackler remembered seeing another such piece about, years agone, and her sought fer 'en high and low. Her found 'en to-last in zome funny place where her least expected. That's why her lookid there, by all accounts.

"So they putt the two bits together and made 'n into a clar'net again. And that was the beginnin' of all the trouble."

2. HOW IT WAS FORMED

"I can't zee why the finding of a li'l thing like a clar'net shude cause a village band, Mr. Elworthy."

"Of cou'se you can't, Mrs. Snell. Can anybody zee why little things shude cause gurt contrastafies? And yet you'll vind it so every day of your life. You might so well say you can't zee why a teeny spark from a ingine shude burn down the whole of wan side of a strate like it did to Orcombe Church-town when dree cottages ketched avire. You might say you can't zee why a li'l small thing like a teen-tack shude upzet a whole church sarvice, same's it did to Zouth Quarridge that Zindy mornin' when zomebody left one stood on its haid in the sate of Varmer Wi'yum Sparley. Varmer Wi'yum weighed purt' near leb'm score, and he was mortle tired with walkin' more 'n two mile to church, so he sot down hard. Thik tack went a gudish ways into Varmer Wi'yum, and tooked a lot o' gettin' out, and in the meantime he made sevver'l remarks which anybody don't hardly expect to yer in such a plaace. So the remainder o' the sarvice wad'n up to the average fer sollumness, cus the volks did'n zeem to be able to ferget it. Although, mind you, more 'n wan o' the congregation was yer'd to say arterwards that if sitch thing was gwain to hap'm very often they'd take to gwain to church rigler.

"So as I say, missis, you can never tell what amount of turmoil a li'l thing is gwain to give rise to. And that's how 'twas with our band. If the tail end o' thik clar'net had a-bin lost, as it shude a-bin lost, and as I wish it *had* a-bin lost, it might a-bin possible to live in Week St. Agnes parish in paice and quietness to this day.

"Even then the wist wude'n have come to

the wist if, when they sticked the clar'net together, it had'n so happened that Zam Blackler putt 'n to his lips, blawed wan puff o' weend into 'en and made a note come. If he had'n made that note come us wude a-bin saved. If only Zammy had blawed and blawed a time or two and nothin' had'n happened he'd have drowed the ole thing so-fur as he cude zee 'en, and that wude a-bin the end aw't. Mrs. Blackler wude have had back her cannlestick and there'd be 'appy 'omes in Week village to-day where there's nothin' now but envy, hatred and mallish.

"And mind you, Zammy never thought fer one minute he was gwain to make a note come. He properly frightened hiszelf. And 'twas days and weeks bevore he made a note come again. But never mind! He'd done it wance, and Mr. Tolley said 'twas a marvel that anybody shude be able to play the clar'net the fust time of asking. So Zam Blackler got the idaya into his haid that he was a clar'net player bred and born; and when Zammy gets a idaya into his haid nothin' short o' dynamite will get it out.

"As I told 'ee bevore, Tom Tolley is a proper musican. He can play any instrument you mind to putt bevore 'en. So he tooked hold to Zammy's clar'net and he played 'Pop goes the Waisel,' right off, wai'out a note of music ner nort. Mrs. Blackler said arterwards her never yer'd nothin' more lovely. You cude almost yer the clar'net spakin' the words, so her reckoned. Tom said 'twas a wicked shame that a butiful music like that shude be lying away to waste.

" 'For all us knaws,' he said, 'there might be other instruments in the parish hid away like it. Us might be able to rake up enough to make a band.'

" 'I knows where there's one,' says Zammy. 'James Widmore to the post-orfice have got one o' they brassen contraptions all tied up in knats. I ferget what they terms it.'

" 'Would it be a cornet?' says Tommy.

" 'That's right, maister,' says Zammy. 'At laiste, that's one o' the names I've yer'd it called. There has been others. Poor ole Adam Finch what lived in the cottage oppozyte the post-orfice had a whole host o' names fer it, and he use to call 'em out o' the winder all the time James was playing; till the policeman told 'n one day that if he did'n stap using sitch language across the public highway he shude summons 'n up bevore his betters.'

" 'Can James Widmore play the cornet, then?' axed Tom.

" 'He alwis reckoned he cude when he was a young feller. He had two chunes in they days, wan fer Zindys and wan fer wickdays. He use to play 'em rigler out in orchard till wan night zome strangers thought 'twas the ole owl and let fly to 'en with the gun. They did'n shoot 'n, as it happened, but it ruined James's taste fer gude music, and I don't believe he've played the cornet ever since.'

" 'If us have got a cornet player,' says Tom, 'that's half the battle.'

"So off he goes to James Widmore and inquired about the cornet. James had 'most fergot all about 'n.

" 'I have'n zee'd 'en this vive-'n-twenty year fer certin, maister,' he says; 'and I wude'n say I cude putt my hand on 'en, not to a minute's notice. Praps my missis knows where 'tis to.'

"When the thing was discribed to Mrs. Widmore her recollected the last place her zee'd 'n to was up in tallet, 'pon-tap the wall, in under the roof. Her noticed 'n there wan day when her was seekin' fer hen's-nesses. And that's where James and Tom vound 'n to. Purt' near buried in muck he was, and lookin' proper vulty you mid be sure.

" 'Try if you can blaw 'en, James,' says Tommy, and he putt his own eye to the big end, to zee if he cude zee any music comin' out. So James tooked a gude puff at 'n. But, o' cou'se, the ole cornet was chuckful of dist and dirt and all manner of rummage, so he blawed a proper cloud in Tommy's faace and the organist was caughin' and splutterin' and spittin' fer the next half-hower.

"However, when they managed to clear out the muck James found he cude blaw 'en all right, and he played a chune. Whether 'twas his Zindy wan or his wickaday wan 'twas impossible to say, zac'ly; 'cus arter all they years the feller had lost the nick aw't a bit. Still, there 'twas, and Tom Tolley considered he was gettin' on like a houze avire.

"'If us cude only get wan or two more musics, James,' he says, 'us cude start a band.'

"'There did use to be a band in the parish years agone,' says James. 'A very gude band, too, by all accounts. I've yer'd my vather say when he was a li'l boye there wad'n nothin' to aiqual it fer miles around. And his vather told he, that when Quane Victoria fust sot on the throne Week village was the only place in the distric' where they was able to play "God Save the Quane."'

"'Well, then, there mus' be zome more musics about zomewhere.'

"'Must, fer certin, unless they'm all broke. Lemme zee,' says James, 'there's Sid Burridge, the blacksmith. His vather use to play the euphonian, and when Sid was a young chap he tooked a very gude hand to it hiszelf. I've yer'd Sid play " Now the day is over " scores o' times, so's anybody cude tell in a minute what chune 'twas. " Amen," and all.'

" Tom Tolley was gettin' properly excited by thees time. He cude zee a band comin' all right with he hiszelf sticked up in front wagglin' a li'l stick about, like they do's it up in Lunnon and down Plymouth.

" ' A band is a vine thing fer a parish, James,' he says. ' It gives the volks zummin to think about and talk about. There's nothing improves the mind so much as music. In the place where I lived to bevore I come yer us had a butiful band with gold lace all around their hats and rid stripes down their trousers. They was a sight only to zee, James, never mind about their music. And I've knowed the times when they chaps has putt as much as vifteen shullins or a pound in their pockets the end o' the wick, only droo playin' about to wan place and another.'

" ' You mid depend music is a very nice 'obby,' says James, ' and I only wish I'd presevered with it instead o' jackin' it up when I did. I shude a-bin able to play ever so many chunes by now. But when a body gets mistook fer owl it makes 'ee wonder what's gwain to hap'm next.'

" ' You shude a-sticked to it till you was

mistook fer a nightingale, James,' says Tom. 'Be-as-'twill, us'll go and zee Sid Burridge.'

"So they went to the blacksmith.

"'Sid, they tells me you use to play the euphonian once,' says the organist. 'Is that right?'

"'Let bygones be bygones, Mr. Tolley,' says the blacksmith. 'Us have all done zummin fulish in our young days, and 'tid'n fair to go hatchin' that up arter all these years.'

"'Have 'ee still got 'en?'

"'Missis have got 'en about zome-place, I believe. When us was courtin' her used to say I played 'n lovely. But zoon arter us got married her decided to take charge aw'n, and her've kep' 'n ever since.'

"'What's that you'm sayin' about me?' says Mrs. Burridge. Her was right out in back-houze when us started talkin', but her come in like a shat when her name was mentioned. Us wad'n spaikin' very loud, nuther. But women is wonderful like that.

"'I was axin' your husband about the euphonian he had wance, Mrs. Burridge,' says Tom Parkhouze.

"'I did'n know he ever had it,' her says. 'He had a titch o' the pewmonium about o' vive year agone. I expec' that's what you'm thinkin' about. And only hiszelf to blame, too, fer he *wude* laive off his flannel shurt in May month although I beggid of 'en not to do anything so fulish. I warned 'n what the result wude be, but he wude'n harken to me, same's he alwis don't. And what was the result? Zix wicks in bed, same's I prophesied. But that was the pewmonium, Mr. Tolley, not what you said. And started with indigestion o' the lungs.'

"So Tom explained what he meant by euphonian.

"'Aw! That noising ole nuisance! I'll tell 'ee what I uses he for, and he do's very well for't, too. I uses he fer growin' bulbs een. I've got 'arrisons in 'en, now.'

"And so her had, begad. And her wude'n hear about shiftin' of 'em, nuther, not till James spoke about the vifteen shullins or a pound a wick. Her soon found a fresh place fer the bulbs, tho.

"'If 'tis gwain to be any benevit to 'en that's a differ'nt matter,' her says. 'And there's wan gude thing about it. If he uses up all his weend tryin' to blow that crooked piece o' trumpery out straight he won't have none left to go finding fault with everything about the place, same's he do now. Only, I tell 'ee wan thing. He shan't come in house with his ole snorin' and snortin', and groanin' and belvin'; cus I cude'n enjure it. If he wants to make they ole noises he mus' go out in linney and make 'em, or zome place further off where I can't yer 'en. Fer it gives me the stommick-ache, Mr. Tolley, and 'tis no gude me turnin' over the dictionary to find fancy names fer it. Gives me the stommick-ache that wearisome noise do, and I may so-well say it as think it. I putt up with it fer zix months arter us was fus' married, cus the poor feller thought he was givin' me a trate with his music, and I did'n want to hurt his veelings. But he beginned to hurt mine, and to-last it come to the pitch when human nature cude'n stand it no longer. Bezides, no less than ten times, fust and last, I went out to turn the cow out o' the garden; and that was he up in the bedrume playin' "The Vacant Cheer," on his ole whatever you said it was.'

"However, that was settled to Mrs. Burridge's satisfaction, and next they went to call upon Bill Bennett cus James and Sid both remembered that Bill's vather use to have a trambone. You know, wan o' they come-to-me go-from-me things. They cude mind seein' the ole feller when they was boyes, puttin' wan end in his mouthe and glidin' tother end back and vore. And wance, when he was playin' a chune into the Rid Lion he tried to reach a note that was extry long way off and shoved the tail of his trambone clane droo the winder.

"When they got to Bill's place they vound the trambone had bin tooked abroad these years and Mrs. Bennett was usin' the big half fer fillin' the washin'-tub. It saved her all that liftin' about cus her cude rin the watter from the pump into the tub wai'out taking aw'n off the stool. Where the other part was to, her cude'n think fer ever so long; but they vound 'n to-last. Her'd got 'n trigged up across a hole in the chicken's house to keep the big hens from gwain in droo. He wad'n hurted a turrable lot, and arter a bit o' trouble they managed to get the ole trambone together so's he'd go in and out if you push 'n hard nuff.

"By thees time Mr. Tolley was jumpin' fer joy, cus he considered he'd got sufficient musics to start a band."

3. THE FIRST NOTE

"There's a gude many volks in Week village can remember the fust night us had a band practice. Matter o' fac', I doubt if there's very many can ferget it, although they wude if they cude.

"Bezides bein' so lucky in the matter o' vindin' all they musics lied about in the different houses in the village Tom Tolley discovered that

Peter Sillage had got a big drum with wan zide almost so-gude as new. There was a biggish hole in tother zide, 'tis true, but Mrs. Sillage is very handy with the needle, and her stitched a piece o' calicoo over that one so's he answered very well so-long as you did'n go knockin' aw'n the wrong zide. The ole drum tooked a bit o' shinin' up, cus he'd bin lied up in Peter's loft fer ages, and the ole cat had made a rule of havin' her kittens in 'en. But when he'd bin clained off and polished up with a-plenty o' bees-wax and turpentine he looked rale smart.

"There use to be a proper stick to scat 'n with back-along, but he was lost long ago. Missis employed 'n fer years clainin' the inside of lamp chimleys and sitch like cus he was handy to push in around. Then the sauft part got all weared out and the hannle was used to fasten the door o' the pig's-looze. Then he was lost sight of and nobody knowed what become of 'n.

"However, they considered 'twude be aisy job to fake up a new drum-stick with a bit o' shammy-leather stuffed with rags and tied on tight to the hannle of a old timbern spoon. But 'twad'n so simple as they thought. 'Twas all right if Peter went along suant, but when he got excited and started latting into the drum as if he was tryin' to knock it up over the mune the knob wude work loose and the stuffin' fly out in the middle o' the chune. Then Zammy wude say 'twas impossible to go on tryin' to play a waltz if Peter was gwain to bate his drum in rag-time.

" By all accounts there shude a-bin a triangle zome-place belongin' to Dicky Maggs. But Mrs. Maggs had used that one years ago to hang up the kettle to the bar over the kitchen vire. He done butiful while he lasted, but he got burned out to-last and was drowed away. However Sid Burridge did'n make nothin' to turn out a new triangle. He had a bit of ire, 'bout so-big around as yer little vinger and hat 'n to shape on his anvil. Sid said if there wad'n no more in makin' fiddles than there was in makin' triangles he'd jack up blacksmithin' and start a music shop. 'Twad'n a very sweet-soundin' triangle I did'n fancy. 'Twas more like anybody dingin' the tongs with the poker, and spoiled the chunes in my estimation. But Tom Tolley said us cude'n have a proper band wai'out a triangle, so us had to have wan ; same's you got to have apple-sass with roast pork and ing'ens, which makes me sick and ruins gude food to my way o' thinkin'.

" Anyway, Tom Tolley reckoned he'd got the makings of a band, seein' they'd scraped up a cornet, a euphonian, a trambone, a clar'net, a drum and a triangle. And he managed to get hold to another cornet to play hiszelf; though what they wanted two vor, considerin' the amount o' noise they cude make with wan, I can't think.

"So the band had their fus' practice up to the raidin' rume. Not in the big rume of course. There's a little off rume, spaused to be fer anybody what wants to get away quiet by theirzels. 'Twas jis' a nice size, so that's where the band had their practice to.

"'Twas of a Wainsdy aiv'min. I know 'twas, cus Varmer Joe Sage had took back a cow and calve from Barleycombe market the zame day. Varmer was sot in the corner o' the settle into the Rid Lion having a li'l drop o' geen and chatting with wan and tother when the band striked up their fus' note, and he jumped up like a man shot.

"'I'm jiggered if that beggerin' cow and calve have'n got out and gone to road.' And away-to-go, coosing down the strate like a long-dog.

"What Varmer did say when he discovered what the noise was I wude'n like to tell 'ee, with ladies present and all. And the buty aw't was, a wik or two later they called up to his houze and beggid fer a suscription towards the band. So then he made the zame remarks over again with a vew extry tettivations which he'd thought out in the meantime."

"Was you there to the practice, Mr. Elworthy?" axed Mrs. Snell.

"What do 'ee mean, 'Was I there?' Did'n I tell you I was appointed foreman triangler, and continued as sitch till I whacked me thumb and spoked out o' me turn? I shude think I *was* there; and when I fergets it 'twill be time to send fer Bob Stooks the undertaker to come and take my measurements.

"Half-pas' zeb'm, Wainsdy aiv'min; that was the instructions. And if anybody fergot 'em they only had theirzelf to blame, fer us was told times enough. Mr. Tolley told us on the Zindy mornin' gwain into church, and he told us again comin' out. To they what was sittin' in the zinging-sates he passed around a bit o' paper during the sarvice with the notice wrote down in big letters.

"Zindy aiv'min he told it all over again to they what was to church, and axed 'em to pass it on to they what wad'n.

"Mondy mornin' he went around to each wan separate to make sure they had'n fergot, and if he ketched sight of wan of 'ee, out about, if 'twas two vields off he'd 'olley out:

"'Don't ferget, mind. Wainsdy aiv'min half-pas' zeb'm.' Or it might be 'zeb'm-thirty' fer a change, but otherwise 'twas identical. And whenever he passed by any of our houses he'd look in and tell our wives to be sure and zee us did'n ferget the band-practice half-pas' zeb'm Wainsdy aiv'min. I tell 'ee, Mr. Tolley was some excited."

"I don't suppose the rest of 'ee was very much better," says Mrs. Snell.

"I wude'n say us was, missis. Spesh'ly they what had what I calls the chune musics. Of course, with regards to the triangle he did'n require very much ambition 'cus you cude'n play but the wan chune, no matter what you done with 'n. When I fus' carr'd 'n home I jis' tried 'n over a bit and I cude zee there wad'n very much to larn, so I putt 'n on wan zide till the practice. Even then I managed to cause a bit of upset. My missis was upstairs to work, and her did'n know 'twas me practisin' the triangle. Her thought 'twas the kitchen clock strikin' twelve and her rished down over the stairs and set the dinner gwain half-a-nower sooner than what her ordained. Her was some mad I can tell 'ee when her discovered the rights o' the matter. Her reckoned it putt her all out fer the rest o' the day. Or whether twad'n the rest o' the week I dunnaw.

"However, Wainsdy aiv'min half-pas' zeb'm arrived, and the band turned up in full force at quarter after eight, which wad'n so bad considerin'. Tom Tolley arranged us all in our proper order.

"Fus' come James Widmore with his cornet, and then Zammy Blackler with his clar'net, then Bill Bennett stood corner-ways so's he cude shove out his ole trambone without knockin' the things about; then come me with the triangle, and Peter Sillage was putt back behind with his big drum where he'd have plenty of elbow rume. Tom being the bandmaster was stood out in front where he cude waggle his li'l stick with wan hand and blow his cornet with tother.

"'Now then,' says Tommy; 'fust thing I wants 'ee all to do is to blow "A."'

"'A what?' says Zammy.

"'Why, "A," yer fule! You knows what "A" is, daun' 'ee?'

"'Yaas. I've got two vields aw't lied out there spoilin', now this very minute. Been cut a vortnit, and rained every day ever since.'

"'Don't be redec'lus,' says Tommy. 'I wants 'ee all to make "A" on yer musics.'

"'Too late in the day, maister,' says Sid Burridge. 'I've alwis been told shude make hay while the zin shines.'

"'Aw, well, of course,' says bandmaster, 'if you *won't* do it proper 'tis useless fer me to try.'

"'What is it you wants, maister?' says

Zammy. 'I'm willin' to do anything I can pervided you tells me what I've got to do.'

" ''Tis notes I wants,' says Tommy. 'You knows the notes I suppose.'

" 'I knows a ten-shullin note, and I know a pound note; and I dersay I shude know a vive-pound note, but I daun' zee they very often.'

" 'Now, look yer,' says ban'master. 'Try and have a bit o' sainse. When I counts, "Wan, two, dree," I wants 'ee to play a note on your musics all together. I shall play note "A" on my cornet, so if you plays the same note as what I be, you'll be playing "A" likewise. Peter must give dree gude scats to his drum, and George Elworthy'—that was me—'is to dingle-dingle on his triangle till I holds up wan hand fer 'ee to stap. Now then; be all ready? Wan, two, DREE.'

" My hyvers! What happened then 'tis impossible fer me to discribe. I never yer'd nothin' like it bevore, and I hope plaise God I never shall again. They chaps tooked in all the breath they cude contain, and when they got the word to go they blowed enough weend into they instruments to sail a big ship from Jerusalem to Jericho. Whether they blowed 'A,' or whether they blowed 'Z,' they did'n know; and they did'n care. They blowed the fust note they come to, and they blowed 'n so that he shude never want blowin' again. The winders rattled in their frames and the picshers on the walls stood out and flapped like flags in a gale. The walls went in and out, but the roof stopped on, and that was a miracle. When 'twas finished and the noise died away us cude yer all the li'l pigs in the parish answering back.

" I said to Tom, ' Wude you call that a small " A " or a cabical " A," Mr. Tolley ? '

" Peter Sillage said, ' If that's only " A," laurd help us when us gets down about " F " or " Q." '

" But the ban'master was very plaised. ' You cude'n expect to get it perfec' the fust time,' he says. ' After us have practised it a bit us'll all be in chune.'

" ' Or else in prisin,' says Peter."

" I wish I'd been there and heard 'ee," says Mrs. Snell. But George jumped around as if her'd said zummin out o' place.

" Don't 'ee say such foolhardy thing, Mrs. Snell. 'Tis temptin' providence to wish anything o' the sort. 'Twad'n nothing that a Christian body cude want to harken to, and I hope I shall never hear you say such thing again. You ax anybody that lives to Week village and they'll tell 'ee 'twas the wist fright ever they had since they yeard the German guns on Gummet's Moor during the war. Bevore the last o' the noise had daied away the square was full o' volks vrightened out o' their lives; and the mothers which had rished upstairs to protec' their chillern poked their haids out o' the winders and holleyed 'Vire,' and 'Mudder.' But us chaps in the band was very plaised with ourzels, and although I says it as shude'n, I doubt very much whether any six men ever made so much noise bevore, all to wan go.

"Sid Burridge with his euphonian hanged on to his note the longest out o' they with the blowing musics. Of coourse, Sid being the blacksmith is a middlin' hefty chap, with a biggish pair o' lungs, and he was able to take in a greater supply o' weend than the rest aw'm. Zammy Blackler with his clar'net was the fust to give een. But Zammy as you know is the lan'lord to the Rid Lion, so he don't get very much exercise out o' doors; and havin' most of his chest as you might say below the waist, and being, likewise, in the habit of taking a drop in and out more 'n what the average man do who have'n got it alwis handy, he id'n in the best o' condition for long-breathidness. He's a bit gone in the weend, and even now, although he've got more used to it, they've alwis got to give Zammy two short notes in place o' wan long wan. But he done his best, Zammy did, and he sticked at it till he was black in the faace, but he was forced to give in to-last, and it took two quarts to restore what Turney Gurney use to call his equal-Abram.

" James Widmore with his cornet was the nex' to die out, and 'twas sevver'l minutes bevore James's eyes went properly back in their place again. In fact, I was feared the poor feller had blawed 'em out o' their sockets fer gude, but he had'n luckily. What Bill Bennett wude a-done 'tis impossible to say, but it so happened that he pushed his ole trambone a bit beyond his reach and got the cramp in his right shoulder ; so part of what us mistook fer his music was only Bill singin' out with the pain. Peter Sillage said 'twude be a vine thing if Bill got the cramp every time cus his zingin' was a lot sweeter than his playin'. But Bill said his cramp was better now and if Peter did'n take care he'd prove it to him.

" Mr. Tolley continued with his note ever so long arter James Widmore had jacked it up. I suppose, being the ban'master, he thought he ought to keep it up longest o' the lot, but Sid Burridge bate 'n by ten seconds. Tommy tried to make out that Sid tooked his breath in the middle o' the note ; but Sid offered to take 'n on again fer zixpence a side, so Tommy had to give 'n best. But mind you, Sid wad'n the longest out o' the whole band. Only out o' the weend-blowin' lot; cus me with my ole triangle, I cude a-went on all night, only fer whacking me thumb by mistake. And so cude Peter Sillage with his gurt drum, come to that; although if it had been a match between me and Peter I shude have winned, cus it use to make Peter puffee with so much wollopin'."

4. LEARNING THE SCALES

"While the band was gettin' their breath back again, Tom Tolley made up a bit of a speech about our fust note to show where us went wrong to, and how us cude improve.

"'Fer wan thing,' he says, 'you muzzen go at it quite so rash. It stands to raison, if you uses up all that quantity of weend fer the fust note, where wude you be to if you had to play a whole chune?'

"'I know where I shude be to,' says Zammy. 'In me grave. Daied fer want of breath, same's me vather and me gran'vather bevore me.'

"'I wish I'd brought along my bicycle pump,' says James.

"'Well, now,' says ban'master, 'us'll play "A" again, but not quite to the zame extaint this time. Blow 'n a bit more plum, and George Elworthy must plaise to remember that when he wishes to spaik to his instrument by name 'tis called a " triangle," and not what he said. Now, then: Wan, two, dree.'

" So us played up another ' A ' not hardly so big as the fus' wan, but still a middlin' gude size, and all the owls in the neighbourhood stapped their zingin', cus they was ashamed to make their trumpery li'l noise arter ours. Ban'maister said 'twas a lot better, and reckoned us was gettin' on vine. ' Now us'll play " B," ' he says.

" ' I suppose that'll be more of a buzzin' sort o' noise ? ' says Zammy.

" ' Is it a bumble bee, or a honey bee, maister?' says Sid.

" ' Neether-wan. 'Tis a " gwain-to-bee." Ready ? Wan, two, dree.'

" Caw, my stars! When 'twas all over and the place had done shakin' everybody lookid around as if they was surprised to vind the walls still stood upright. Sid Burridge said, ' I reckon they bees must a-bin swarming.'

" ' Mine was more like a wopse than a bee,' says James; but Zammy considered an elephant was nearer the mark.

" ' 'Twad'n so bad,' says Tommy. ' Us can't expect to get right on the spot very fust go.'

" ' Never mind,' says Bill Bennett, ' us was within hearin' distance, anyway.'

" 'Well, now us have done "B,"' says Mr. Tolley, 'us'll go to "C."'

" 'I'll make a bet there's a gude many in the parish wude be glad if we was to,' says Peter Sillage.

" However, us done 'C,' and then us done 'D,' and right on so-fur as 'G.' By that time things had aised off a bit cus the weend had 'bated a lot.

" 'Now you've larned to do the notes wan to a time,' says Tom, 'I be gwain to putt 'ee on to the scales.'

" 'I'll make a bet I've lost pounds,' says Zammy.

" 'The scales is most important,' says ban'-master, 'and they must be got correct bevore us goes any vurder.'

" ''Ees, begad,' says James Widmore. 'Did 'ee zee what happened only last wik to Wi'yum Shillacott to Barleycombe? The inspector went into his place and found his scales wad'n correct, and Wi'yum had to go up bevore his betters, and I'm popped if he wad'n vined vive pound.'

" But of coorse, it wad'n that sort o' scales, as James knowed very well, only he must try to be funny. Tommy sticked a gurt sheet o' paper up agin the wall with a sort of a ladder marked on it, and a lot o' black spots with long tails like tadpoles gwain up wan side o' the ladder and down tother. He explained that they black spots was the notes, and he larned us which was "A," and which was "B," and so forth. And then he tooked his cornet and blowed all they notes one to a time; and I'm jiggered if you cude'n track 'em up-hill and down-dale while he was playin' of 'em as aisy as you cude track a rabbut in the snaw. When the notes went hup Tommy went hup, and when the notes went down Tommy went down accordin'.

"'I've got the hang aw't,' says James. 'If I'd knowed there was no more than that in playin' music I'd have went in fer't years agone.'

"Ban'master told us to go on tryin' over they notes, each body for hiszelf, till us got accustomed to 'em. So us done that, and 'twas all right so-fur as it went. The trouble was it did'n go fur nuff. What I mean to say, you'm only 'lowed to go so-fur as 'G,' and arter that you'm suppaused to go back to 'A' and start afresh. And of coorse, zome o' the chaps wude keep gwain on to 'H' and bustin' the contract. And on one occasion when Mr. Tolley was paying attention to zome other body Bill Bennett got right down so-fur as 'W' bevore ban'master cude stop 'n.

"'Twas a mercy he hadn' ruined his ole trambone or done hiszelf a injury. But Bill did'n look at it in that light, and instead o' being thankful to the ban'master fer savin' of 'n he showed off his temper, cus he said if he'd only bin allowed to blow dree more notes he'd a-played the whole alphabet.

"However, the next step was fer everybody to all play the zame note to-once, when ban'master pointed to 'en on the paper with his stick. That wad'n so aisy as playin' of 'n wan to a time cus if anybody happened to be on the wrong note it showed up most hawful.

"Of coorse, with me and Peter Sillage it wad'n very much, cus every time us had to play a fresh note 'twas only to do the zame one over again. I cude rattle mine off without so-much as looking to the music. But the chaps with the blowin' musics was in a different box. They had to make a fresh note every time, and it must be similer to what the rest was doing, otherwise 'twude be a ojis noise. Poor ole Sid Burridge with his euphonian zeemed to have properly lost the hang aw't, and 'twas a long while bevore he cude get the right idaya. Every time he was supposed to play a fresh note, instead o' gwain wan higher all he done was to blow the zame wan again a bit harder. So, of coorse, he wad'n in chune with the rest. And, furthermore, after he'd increased to the vorth or vith note, he wad'n capable to putt no more extry weend behind it.

"'I can't go no higher, mister,' he says.

'The tap o' my haid will come off if I blows any harder.'

"Matter o' fac', he was still blowin' the zame note where he started to. The only thing which had gone up any higher was his eyebrows, and they'd gone hup and hup accordin' as he thought he was playin' higher notes, till they was titchin' his hat and cude'n go no vurder.

"Ban'master had all the works in the world to make Sidney understand that he wad'n blowin' no higher, only louder. The amazin' part was if you let 'n go along by hiszelf he'd do it butiful up one side and down tother, as aisy as walkin' on a step-ladder. But direc'ly he got in along o' the rest, zomehow or 'nother he zeemed to lost count.

"Very nearly bust up the ole band, that did, cus the rest o' the chaps, instead o' lettin' the ban'master do all the fau't-findin', they all kep' on tellin' Sid he was all wrong, and he ought to do this and he ought to do that. And of coorse, every time there was a bit of a scummer and they was forced to stap, they all putt the blame on to Sidney. So to-last he beginned to get his wool off. And then when Peter Sillage offered to show Sid what sort o' face he made when he was tryin' to play a high note, that just about putt the finisher on it. Sidney told about puttin' his euphonian down over Peter's haid fer a hat.

And he cude 'a-done it, too, for Peter id'n above half the size o' the blacksmith.

" However, us managed to smooth things over with a little tac', and then with a bit more practice Sid got into the way aw't, so us was able to play the scales butiful.

" I'll admit 'twas a bit of a puzzle zometimes to tell whether us was gwain up or comin' down ; and I dersay if you'd axed eether o' the chaps all of a sudden which note he played last he'd have a job to tell 'ee without adding 'em up on his vingers. But that daun' alter the fac', us played they scales, up and down and vore and back, right zide in and inzide out ; us played 'em loud and us played 'em very loud ; us played they scales till us had blowed 'em right out to a straight line. *And* us was all alive at the finish ; so what cude anybody want more ?

" Us knocked off work fer the night, half-hower bevore closin' time, and a sort of peacefulness zeemed to settle down over the village. But bevore us left the rume Tom Tolley let us have a sheet o' paaper a-piece with all the notes wrote down, so's us cude keep up our practice at home till the nex' meeting. And everybody in the parish said he ought to have had more sense.

" As ole Ned Pugsley putt it, 'Nuff's nuff, but too much is a doost of a lot.'

" Volks reckoned 'twas bad nuff when the

band was all together in the raidin'-rume ; but at any rate they cude excape from the noise by gwain to zome other part o' the parish. Mrs. Tarpitt, what keeps the King's Arms right out to Storget, cude'n understand why her house had suddenly become so pop'ler of a Wainsdy and Saturday aiv'mins. 'Twas only the people tryin' to get so far as possible away from the music.

"But when the band chaps was scattered all about the parish makin' uproar in their own houses all howers o' the day and night, 'twas impossible to avoid it. Bevore you was out o' reach of Sid Burridge's euphonian you was within the scope of Sammy Blackler's clar'net, or James Widmore's cornet. And all blowin' scales as hard as they cude go, cus that's all they'd larned up to now. There's no gettin' away from the fac', 'twas a bomination to they what had to harken to it ; nothing but everlastin' howlin' from A up to G and growlin' back again. Sevver'l people went to the policeman, so I've bin told, to see if zummin cude'n be done in the matter, and Dan Radferd the cobbler even went so far as to threaten to write a letter to the papers about it.

"The most disturbance o' the lot, I railly think, was Bill Bennett with his ole trambone. Being the caretaker to the Insichute and havin' a strong, healthy wife he had'n got nothing to occupy his time. So with the exception of stoppin' fer meals he cude take the whole day fer practising; and that's zac'ly how long he did take. Even his own dog cude'n stand it; and after zingin' to his master's playin' fer two days and a half, the faithful animal what had bin Bill's friend and companion fer ten years went off and was never see'd again.

" So you must imagine what 'twas like for Mrs. Porter, living in the houze next door to the Insichute. With only one wall in between her got the full benefit. Of coorse, Mrs. Porter did'n have the sympathy that some people wude a-got, cus her's a wumman what id'n liked very much, havin' such a long tongue and givin' it so much to do. Her talks so fast that her daun' give herself time to think, and so her very often spaiks the truth when 'twude be a lot more lady-like to keep it dark. So natcherly her id'n very pop'ler, cus 'tid'n many people likes to yer the truth about theirzels wai'out a touch o' varnish. Spesh'ly when they can't get a word in edgeways to return the compliment. Mrs. Porter was drove purt' near wild with Bill Bennett's everlastin' blarin', cus her cude'n make herzelf yeard, not even by her ole man; and that was a turrable blow to the poor wumman, although 'twas a godsend to Bob Porter, who had'n had so much paice from his wive's tongue all the twenty-odd years they'd bin married.

"Her putt up with Bill's scales fer a day or two cus her was convinced that nobody cude go on like it very long without some internal injury. But although Bill id'n very much to look at he've got amazin' strong lungs, and zo he went on blastin' out gurt lumps o' music, up one zide the scale and down tother, till Mrs. Porter was gettin' in a bad way with the stoppage in her spaikin' chubes. Her tried bumpin' on the wall, but that did'n make no differ'nce ; her holleyed remarks out the winder, but her might-so-well 'a-bin blowin' the time off a puff-ball. Bill went on tearin' the notes out of his ole trambone, becus he was determined to master they scales or die in the attemp'. And he did'n die in the attemp', although Mrs. Porter said if her only had a gun he wude 'a-done.

"And when her cude'n tolerate it no longer her went and knacked to Bill's door. Mrs. Bennett went out.

"'Will you plaise to spaik to that husband o' yours about this idjis noise he's makin'?'

"'You spaik to 'en yerzelf. He waun' harken to me.'

"'You zend 'en out yer. I'll let 'n know.'

"So Bill went out, trambone and all.

"'I shude like to know how much longer you

thinks you'm gwain to continue kickin' up that 'orrible row, Mr. Bennett.'

"'Row, Mrs. Porter! What do 'ee mean, row! Let me tell you, that's music.'

"'Music be blowed.'

"'That's right, missis. And takes a deal o' blowin', too,'

"'Well, tid'n worth the trouble.'

"'No trouble at all, missis. 'Tis a pleasure.'

"''Tis no pleasure to me, let me tell 'ee.'

"'That's cus you ab'm got ear for music, Mrs. Porter. If I daun't practise I shall never larn to play, shall I?'

"You daun't have to larn to make that noise. Any fule cude do that without larnin'. What you wants to do is to larn not to.'

"''Tid'n true,' says Bill. 'It takes a lot o' doing to slide 'n in and out zacly the right place. You watch me and you'll zee.'

"And with the zame he ups with his ole trambone, aimed 'n straight to Mrs. Porter and started to blow. Her scraimed at 'n to the tap of her voice, and the more her holleyed the more he blowed. 'Twas the fust thing her'd ever come across that her cude'n demolish by talking. I'd back her agin any man or wumman this side o' Lunnon, but her wad'n the aiqual of Bill Bennett's trambone.

"Bill played his 'A,' 'B,' 'C' vore and back,

up and down and in and out. Mrs. Porter's mouth was workin' like a drashin' machine, but not a sound cude be yeard above the din. All of a sudden her turned right around and rished off to the policeman.

" 'I daun't see what I can do about it, missis,' said the policeman.

" 'He's makin' hiszelf a nuisance, and therefore you ought to lock 'n up.'

" 'Nonsense, missis. If I was to lock up everybody what makes theirzelf a nuisance I shude have enough to do. Best thing you can do is to go to the Squire about it, 'cus he'm a magistrate.'

" And I'm beggered if her did'n, too. Squire said he wude zee what he cude do in the matter, and the zame arternune he met with Robert Porter.

" 'Of coorse, Porter,' he saith, 'if your wive's determined to take it to coort I'm bound to let 'ee have a summons, but 'tis a pity to have sitch table-talk in the parish.'

" 'Well, yer honour,' says Bob, 'I tell 'ee straight, if it comes to a coort job I shall go witness for Bennett, and I shall swear that tid'n no nuisance.'

" Caw, did'n Squire laaf!

" 'In that case 'tis no gude you havin' a summons. So you likes the music, do 'ee?'

" 'Tid'n to say I likes the music, yer honour. But 'tis eether that or my wife's tongue, and havin' had vive-and-twenty years o' the tongue I'm willin' to have the trombone fer a change.' "

5. THE FIRST TUNE

" Playin' a chune," says George, " is a very differ'nt thing to playin' notes one to a time. To make a chune you've got to understand music. What I mean to say, you've got to be able to volley they li'l black long-tails wherever they goes to. If they goes up high you must go up high, and if they goes down low you must drop down accordin'.

" Us held our fust chune-practice Zaturday night, so's to have Zindy to get over it. 'Twas my last performance with the band, cus in the excitement of playin' chunes I scat my thumb to such extent that the ban'master said I'd be sure to repeat the zame remarks if us was playin' in public, and 'twude get the band a bad name. So I handed over the triangle to Ernie Meers, who's a taicher in the Zindy-skule.

" You zee, there's another thing about chune-music which makes it more ticklish than playin' scales, and that is, you ban't all playin' the zame notes. When 'tis only scales you knows very well if you ban't makin' the zame noise as the chap next to 'ee one of 'ee must be wrong, and so you harkens to the rest and goes by the majolity. But when 'tis chunes you can't do that, cus you'm all supposed to be doin' differ'nt. One's playin' the tribble and another the allto and zomebody else is on with the tinner and Bill, with his ole trambone, is puttin' in the baze. So instead of all gwain one way, as you might zay, you'm blowin' one again tother. One feller might be makin' a 'B' or a 'F' and praps the chap nex' to 'en wude be blowin' a 'G' or a 'X' if 'twas allowed.

"Each musican had a bit o' paper to hiszelf with all his notes marked out, and no two alike. It shows what a wonderful haid-piece Tom Tolley must have to be able to sketch out all they sheets o' paper for the differ'nt musics so's it shude all come right in the end. He let us each have our right piece o' paper and us got ready to make a start.

"'This is a aisy chune,' he says. 'I didn't want to give 'ee nothing too difficult fust start off. Us mus' walk bevore us can rin.'

"'If us do's the walkin' the volks outzide will do the rinnin' fast nuff,' says Sid Burridge.

"'Which is the correc' way up of my music, maister?' says Bill Bennett. 'He don't zeem right eether-one o' the ways.'

" 'If you keeps the han'writin' to the top where it says the name of yer instrument, you'll be all right.'

" 'I thought that wude be it, most likely,' says Bill, 'but it don't look vitty, zomehow. Did'n they li'l black fellers ought to have their tails all one way? Some's pokin' up fer vine weather and some's hangin' down like the hannle o' the pump.'

" 'It daun' make a bit of odds to the chune which way the tails is pointin',' says ban'master.

" 'No,' says Bill, 'I did'n suppose it made any odds. I only thought it looked untidy, that's all.'

" 'Now,' says Mr. Tolley, 'I wants 'ee all to look to Mr. Blackler's music fer a minute, cus he've got what us calls the air, or the chune if you like to term it so. Can any of 'ee tell what chune 'tis by lookin' at it?'

" Us all gappid to Zammy's paper. Sid Burridge said: 'Jidgin' by the look aw't I shude say 'twas the chune what killed the cat.'

" 'No,' says Peter Sillage, ' 'tis the chune the dunkey died of.'

" 'If that's the case,' says James Widmore, 'how is it you daun' drop daid?'

" 'Nobody cude'n tell the chune by lookin' to they spots, cude 'um, maister?' says Zammy.

" 'Anybody cude what was accustomed to

music,' says Tommy. 'However! Us'll zee what you can do wai't. You'll notice the fust eight notes is all zac'ly alike.'

"'So they be,' says Zammy. 'If a feller got started proper he ought to be able to manage that rap all right.'

"'What notes be 'um, Mr. Blackler?'

"'Lemme zee, Mr. Tolley. They'm on the second rung from the bottom o' the ladder. That wude be 'G,' wude'n it?'

"'That's right. So you've got eight 'G's' to start wai'.'

"'Two pairs of hosses,' says Peter.

"'What nonsense be you talkin' about now?'

"'Wull, eight gees is vower gee-gees.'

"'Daun't you be so flighty,' says Zammy. 'This matter have got to be took sayrious. That's right, Mr. Tolley. There's eight along on the flat and one up over the jump and then one down in the ditch and then one up over again.'

"'Wull, now, zee if you can play that lot on yer clar'net, and mind you keep the right time. 'Tis the time us have got to keep our eye upon. Time is half the battle.'

"'Very true, maister,' says Peter. 'Half-past nine is rinnin' it a bit close. By the time us have raiched the Rid Lion and been sarved a body have hardly got chance to get a proper drink.'

" 'I shude have thought you'd have had more sense,' says Zammy, 'than to go talkin' about drinks jist as I be gwain to try to blow.'

" So they sticked up the music where Zammy cude zee it and he tooked in a gude supply o' weend and started knockin' off they 'G's.' Halfways over he stapped.

" 'How many did you say 'twas?'

" 'Eight, Zammy. They'm all there on the paper.'

" 'Yes, I zee they be.'

" So he started again, blowed a vew times and stapped with the zame.

" 'Have I done eight?'

" 'No, ti-no. You ab'm done but zix. Why daun' 'ee watch yer notes?'

" 'I *be* watchin' 'em, but I can't keep count o' the li'l toads, cus drec'ly I starts to blow they goes dappin' about all over the shop.'

" 'That'll come to 'ee all right when you gets better used to it,' says Tommy. 'You wants to keep cule. Have another go at 'n and not be so aiger.'

" So Zammy went fer 'n again, and this time he rattled right past the station. Everybody started holleyin'.

" 'Whoa! Way! Get back! You've done ten a-ready.'

" 'I ab'm, have I?' he says. 'There's dree

more out to the end I'll swear I ab'm played yet. I must 'a-done zome aw'm over twice.'

"However, Tom Tolley said he'd count fer 'n, and so Zammy done his eight 'G's' to-last.

"'Go on, Zammy, you'm doin' butiful,' he says, proper excited. 'One up, now one down, now one up again.'

"When Zammy had played his line, ban'-master said, 'Now can 'ee tell what chune 'tis?' But nobody cude'n putt a name to it.

"'Play 'en over again, Zammy," says James. 'Us was so abzorbed in they 'G's' us did'n take proper count o' the chune.'

"So Zammy done it again; but it did'n zound like nothing us knowed. Us guessed everything us cude think of, from 'Uncle Tom Cobley' to 'God zave the King,' to try to plaise Mr. Tolley, but nobody guessed right.

"'I'll play 'n over mezelf in his proper time,' he says; and with the zame he picks up his cornet and rattles 'n off. And my dear zaul, what a differ'nce it made. Us had 'n in a minute.

"'Jeremiah blow the Vire!' Us all holleyed it out in one breath.

"'That's it,' says maister.

"'I knaw it was,' says Bill Bennett. 'Caw, darn 'ee, I cude yer the words as plain as if maister was zinging 'em:

" Jeremiah, blow the Vire,
Puff, puff, puff,
Fust he blowed 'n gently,
Then he blowed 'n rough." '

" 'Now the rest of 'ee must larn yer parts and then us'll putt 'em all together,' says Tom, 'and make a chune of it.'

" Us made zummin of it, but whe'er 'twas a chune or no I wude'n like to zay.

" Bill Bennett's bit on the trambone wad'n very much. 'Twad'n but two differ'nt notes all told, one high one and one low one. But you'd never believe the trouble ole Bill had to fit 'em in their proper places. He'd eetherways be one short with the high notes or one too many, and then of coorse his low notes wude be all used up bevore us come to the end o' the chune, or else he'd have one or two left over when all the rest had finished; and instead o' keepin' 'em quiet as he shude 'a-done, he wude insist on playin' 'em right out to the bitter end. Natcherly, it spoilt the whole effec' havin' him gwain on with two or dree more grunts arter the thing was spaused to be done with.

" Sid Burridge did'n make very much of a fist with his department. But Sid's a hefty gurt feller and you cude'n keep on tellin' him he was wrong else he was ap' to get nasty; so it had to go to that. James Widmore got on purty well, and of coorse, me and Peter did'n require very much practisin' cus ours was all the zame over again fer a change.

" And when us had larned our parts one to a time the ban'master said us shude play all together.

" 'I shall count vower this time. Be all ready? One, two, dree, Go!'

" Us went. Jeremiah and all. I'll make a bet you never yer'd the equal to it in all your born days. There never was sitch a chune played bevore and never will again. Us started off together, but arter that us never zee'd one-tother no more. Zome went away at the gallup, neck or nort, over hedges and ditches; others went more cautious and remembered their wives and vamilies. Zammy rattled off his eight 'G's' and gudeness knows what happened to 'en then, but I noticed he was graj'ly gettin' more and more of his clar'net into his mouthe. Sid Burridge gived a imitation of a cow with a sore throat, and a very gude imitation, too. James Widmore was playin' zummin, but 'twad'n 'Jeremiah.' As fer me and Peter, us was prepared to go on as long as there was anybody left in; Peter lerrickin' his ole drum as if he was choppin' down a tree, and me hattin' the triangle and me awn thumb, turn and turn about.

"Ban'master was fust past the post. That was only to be expected, him bein' a proper musicker. Of the rest James Widmore reckoned he was the winner, and there was turrable argiment between him and Zammy cus Zammy said James had chaited.

"'You did'n do all the puffs, James,' he says.

"'Yas I did, Zammy. I puffed dree times.'

"'No, you did'n, you never puffed but twice.'

"Sid Burridge tried to make out that he finished long ago, only when he vound nobody else had'n come to the end he started again, and that's why he came in last. Bill Bennett was out o' the hunt altogether, cus when he come to his low note he pushed his ole trambone all abroad and cude'n get 'n together again in the time.

"Mr. Tolley said there was one comfert; us was bound to improve on it. So us played our chune again; and us played 'n a dizzen times. Or it might be a score. Be-as-'twill, us sticked to 'en till us reckoned us had got 'n perfect. And then us left work and went home.

"And the instant us putt our haids in around the door to the Rid Lion they was all around us like flies.

"'Come on, you chaps,' they said, 'you'm wanted in yer. Us have got a bet on between Walter Arris and Georgie Paddon over the chune you've bin playin.' Walter have bet George 'twas "While Shepherds Watched," and George have bet Walter 'twas " The Varmer's Boy," So now you can settle it. Which was it ? '

" If you daun't think that was nuff to break the heart of anybody what had bin blowin' his inside out fer two mortle howers, then I dunnaw what is. 'Twas nuff to make anybody say he wude'n do nothin' more fer the benevit of the public. Anyway, so-fur as I was consarned 'twas the last beat in the bar.

V

WHEN JAN WENT FLYING

THEY said to me, " Jan, wude you like to go fer a ride in airyplane? "

Haw, my dear days! Wude I like to go fer ride in airyplane!

How many times had I stood there with me heart comin' up in me mouthe only to watch the 'mazing tattics o' those fellows up in the air. There was a time when 'twas thought to be zummin' wonderful fer a flyin' chap to go loopin' the loop. Now, begad, he'll turn his ole machine upzide-down only to get his matches out from his pocket.

'Most every day I used to zee 'em carr'ing on with their fulish capers, cus us was pra'tically nex' door to the Flying Corpse And I got to know sevver'l o' the chaps to spaik to. Very gude chaps they was, too, when they was walkin' about in a sensible fashin'. But what outrageous manoovers they wude be up to drec'ly they got up in the air.

They'd ride their ole machines vorrads and

back'erds, zideways, up-'n-down or in-'n-out; they'd make 'em spin like a top or go round like the 'obby-'osses; they'd make 'em 'op-skip-an'-jump, rear up, lie down, roll over, tie theirzels up in knots, rin around arter their tails, sit up and beg, stand on their haid, waltz, poker, shotteeze, turn a zummerzet—do any mortle thing barrin' talk. They'd go right up to the sky till they wad'n no more than a spicket and then fall down like a dead burd, fust wan side and then tother, till you must shut yer eyes not to zee the poor feller scat all abroad to flibbits. And jis' when you'd think he had'n but one more minute to live the ole airyplane wude stap short, pull hiszelf together, look around, and away-da-go like a hawk.

And then they said to me, "Jan, wude'n you like to go fer ride in a airyplane?"

"Yaas," I said; "when the pigs flies then you might zee Jan Stewer flyin', but not bevore."

"The Almighty let me have two veet," I says, "same purpose to walk about 'pon-tap the floor. If it had bin ordained fer me to go up there along o' the zin by day and the mune and the stars by night I shude 'a-bin provided with wings like a duck. Ducks can't fly nothin' to boast about, but if me and a duck was to start off together from a airyplane I shude fancy his chance a lot better than what I wude mine. I dersay I shude get down fust, but I reckon he'd vinish in the better condition.

But it jis' shows 'ee what poor fules us men-volk be. Wan vine mornin' I was stood gappin' to the ole airyplanes and there was one stood by all in readiness to go up. Bim-by the chap come out what belonged to 'en and when he zee'd me he said :

" Ullaw, Jan. Be you comin' up fer a ride. 'Tis a butiful day fer't."

And what ever possessed me I dunnaw ; ner I can't think. But I lookid to he and I lookid to the ole airyplane. And he was a vine upstandin' feller as ever vore butes, with his leathern coat and hat and his funny sparticles up over the tap of his haid. A merry-lookin' face he had like a sunny mornin', and a twinkle in his eye that shude 'a-made me more cautious.

" Thank-'ee, zur. If you mind to have me I shall be plaised to come."

Bigger lai never was uttered ; but the words was said bevore I hardly knowed what I was tellin' about. They zeemed to come out o' me mouthe by theirzels and I was frightened to yer 'em.

" Come on, then," he saith, and off he goes, me volleyin' after the tail aw'n, wonderin' what I'd done and whether 'twas too late to alter it or no.

Us went over across to where his ole contraption was stood to. Tremenjis heighth he zeemed when I got close to 'en, and a sight bigger than what I thought. Like a hugly gurt grass-hopper he looked, with wheels fer legs, and the gurt wings aw'n spread out all ready to vly away with me soon's ever I got inside.

"Go on, Jan; clim' up," said the air chap.

"Pilot," they calls 'en. Whe'er 'tis short fer Ponshus Pilot or no I can't say, but I shude think it ought to be.

"I dunnaw so much about climmin' up, young man," I says. "I ban't so flippant as what I use to be.'"

However, one started pullin' above and a couple pushed up below and they shoved me in over the zide into the back sate.

'Tis a funny li'l ole place when you'm in there. You'm sot down so low, only yer haid pokes up over the zide. I was very glad o' that cus there wad'n so much likelihudes o' valling out over. And you ab'm got no rume to go scammellin' yer feet about, nuther, cus there's all manner of hannles and gadjets there which you muzzen touch 'pon no account.

Pilot warned me most pa'ticler about they. "When us be flyin'," he saith, "they hannles will move about, and if you gets in the way aw'm us'll very likely come down quicker than what us intended."

Laur massey. I never watched nothing so keen in all my life as what I did they hannles. If they'd bin kings and quanes I cude'n have paid more rispect to 'em.

The nex' thing they done was to putt a leathern cap on me haid and tie 'n in under me chin with two bits o' coord like gran'mother's bonnet. There was two injy-rubber pipes belongin' to this-yer cap, and they was attached to the side of the airyplane. I considered that was to prevent me from lainin' me haid too fur out over the side. The idaya was all right I dersay, but they'd no cause to be anxious. There wad'n very much fear o' me lainin' out over. Once I sot down I was about as lissom as a gun-barreel.

Then a feller made fast a gurt leathern strap around me waist. 'Tis a quare sinsation, I can tell 'ee, to think you'm in a place where they've got to putt a kickin'-strap around 'ee to keep 'ee from fallin' out. I thought to mezelf, "Spausin' the ole girth was to break! Where shude I be to then?" And I ketched hold to thik strap, my dear, with both hands, like a drownin' man hangin' on to a stick, and I never let go 'n fer wan instant 'genst 'twas all over. I'll make a bet I cude pick out thikky strap from a thousand, cus the marks o' my vinger-nails mus' be in 'en to this day.

Mr. Pilot he clim'ed up into the airyplane and sot down in front o' me like as if he meant business. And then all the things come into me mind that I'd read on the papers about the dreadful accidents which had happened to volks in airyplanes ; and I was glad I'd changed me socks and put on clane underclothes and had a gude bath, cus I knowed that was the fust thing my missis wude ax me. Alwis, if I didn' change me shurt hardly so soon as her thought I ought to, her use to say, " Whatever wude you veel like if you was killed all of a sudden and they was to vind 'ee wearin' a durty shurt ? "

Pilot fiddled about with his hannles fer a bit to make sure they was in workin' order, and there was me behind prayin' hard he'd find zummat wrong wai' 'em, so's us cude'n start. But they was all right, wiss luck. Whenever he moved his hannles about the ones bezide o' me moved likewise, and I thought to mezelf, "That's the idaya, Jan. If you can only vind out which o' they hannles makes the blimmin thing stap you'll be able to stap 'n yerzelf when you've had sufficient."

And then I thought again, " Ees ; and a fat lot o' gude stoppin' of 'n if us be hunderd mile up in the air."

So there wad'n very much in that.

A chap went around in front o' the airyplane and started twistin' around the ole whirligig thing. And all of a sudden he went wizzin' around with sitch a roar and a racket, I shude 'a-jumped clane out o' me sate if it had'n bin fer the ole kickin'-strap.

So I knowed I was in fer it purty quick. What I wude 'a-given to 'a-been ten mile away that very minute; and all the inzide o' me gone holler, like a bladder, and the tap o' me haid and the bottoms o' me veet all pins and niddles.

Pilot made meanings to the chaps what was holding back the airyplane to let 'n go. I tried to holley to 'em to ketch 'n hold again. But I was too late. Us was on the move. Bevore you cude say "knive" the ole contraption was coosin' along the ground like a gurt gander with his wings stretched out and the vox behind 'n. Vaster and vaster us went, and then I zeem to imagine the ole machine was gettin' wonderful tall. And he got taller and taller, like as if the wheels was growin' bigger. So I jus' glimpsed out over the zide to see if 'twas so.

Aw, my dear zaul. Us was up in the air!

I took wan look to zee if there was any hope o' gettin' back, but 'twas too late.

Us was high as a houze.

Us was high as a church.

Us was high as a canthedral.

And us was gwain higher.

'Tis a turrable weesht sinsation, my dear, when you sees the earth and all that therein is, droppin' down and down away from 'ee and nothin' to connect 'ee together.

But there was no way out aw't now. Let come what may, I must bide where I was to, and only too thankful if I was allowed to do that.

After a bit my mind beginned to settle down a bit, like a potful o' boilin' dumplin's took off the vire. And I mus' say, twad'n bad trav'lin'. Her went along a lot more suant than any other vayacle that I ever rode in. Only, of course, you've got the veelin' all the time that if her shude take it into her haid to stap still and go straight home 'twill be very anxious time comin' towards the bump.

But when you do get sufficient courage to look out over the zide, 'tis like a new world, very wonderful to behold. I almost fergot to be frightened I was so took up with the amazement aw't. I cude zee in one view what wude take me weeks to zee if I was on the ground. I tried to pick out the places I knowed. In the town I cude zee the strates, not like I'd bin 'customed to zee 'em, one to a time, but all the lot to-once, marked out like the bars of a gate. The church looked like a lump o' shugger and the gas-works was a couple o' pill-boxes. The sawjer's camp was fer all the gude in the world like a lot o' dripmy-bits lied along on the ground, and the hills was only little want-heaps.

But as I zay, that was all very well so-long as the ole airyplane went along suant and behaved hiszelf in a rispectable manner. 'Twas when he started his ole monkey-tricks that the trouble beginned.

The fust inklin' I had of anything wrong was arter us had flied over the harbour place where the ships was to.

I 'spec' you knows what the wings of a airyplane is like. They'm a tremenjis size when you'm close to 'em, and if you'm sot in the machine up in the air 'tis a sort of comfort to 'ee to see they gurt fellers sticked out one each side of ee'. You'm plaised to have zummin so big and broad and flat, and you knows that so-long as they bides there you'm all right. Wull, as I said bevore, I was lookin' out over the zide and jis' beginnin' to veel a li'l more at home like, when all of a zudden I see'd zummin draidful hap'm. I cude'n believe me eyes. I thought they mus' be desayvin' me. But no! 'Twas only too true. Me heart come right up into me mouthe and I went all over preckles. The hair on me haid stood up like a sweepin' brush, and if me hat had'n bin tied under me chin he'd 'a-went clane off.

That there wing, the only bit o' satisfaction I'd got all up there in the bright blue sky was dippin' downwards at the far end! Slopin' down and down he was, graj'ly towards the ground. And when I turned me haid the other way to zee what was happenin', the oppozyte wing was gwain up!

The darned ole airyplane was tippin' all over to one side; and the ground more 'n a mile away!

What little brains there was inzide me haid started rishin' round and round and fallin' over theirzels. I went hot as vire and cold as ice. I shouted to Pilot to take care, but his ole whirligig was creatin' such a clatter I might jis'-so-well try to talk to the man in the mune. And still us was lainin' over more and more till I was squintin' at the ground out o' the corner of me eye; and all the time tryin' to push the ole airyplane into upright position.

Then zummin' else happened which jist about drove the last bit o' conscience out of me body. Zac'ly as I thought the ole contraption was gwain to topple right over and tip me out I yer'd a loud voice behind me, "Let yerzelf go with the machine."

Behind me, mind!

I tell 'ee straight, if it had'n bin fer the ole kickin'-strap I shude 'a-jumped right out o' me sate. I turned me haid around quick to zee who was talkin' to me *and there wad'n nobody there.*

Aw dear! Aw, dear! I thought to mezelf. "Us have got up so high us be in amongs' the ghostis o' the daid folk; and 'twaun't be very long bevore I'm one of 'em, mezelf."

And with the zame the voice come again. "Let yerself go with the machine."

And then I zee'd where 'twas comin' from. You remember I told 'ee the hat they tied on me haid had a couple o' pipes attached to en'. I thought they was to keep me from lainin' out over. But they wad'n. They was spaikin' chubes, and Mr. Pilot was talkin' down tother end right into my yer'ole.

But aw, my dear. Jus' you think aw't. There was me, right up in the sky, higher than the burds of the air, with nothing as you might say between me and kingdom come in eether derection, the blessid ole contrivance turnin' upzide down, and then zomebody tells me to let mezelf go with the machine. Darn 'ee, I wanted to know where the machine was gwain to fust.

But laur bless yer 'art, that was only the beginnin' of me troubles. When the ole machine had lied over so-fur as he cude go in one direction he took it into his head to tip over tother way. 'Twude'n 'a-bin so bad if I'd been aware what his next intentions was. But all I knowed was that us was gwain through all manner of antics up in the air and I cude'n say fer certain whether us was doin' it on purpose or by accident.

And to crown the lot the heavens above and the earth beneath started to behave theirzels in a most unraisonable manner. The town and the harbour and the deep blue sea and the vields went dappin' about all over the plaace. One minute the houses wude be to the right of me and the hills to the left o' me and the sky up over me haid, in their proper place where they was intended to be accordin' to the tain commandments. And then, all of a sudden, the whole world wude shift. The town wude go rishin'away towards the mountins, the mountins flipped up into the sky, the harbour and ships went coosin' from east to west, the heavens come down on the earth and the earth went up to heaven. Tell about the hills skippin' like young rams! They hopped like ole kangaroons.

Of coorse, I knows very well it was we what was twestin' about and not the firmament. But I'm tellin' you what it zeemed like to me when thik pilot feller started his ole capers.

And mind you, 'tis a very differ'nt thing talkin' it over down yer, sot in a aisy cheer where the most you cude fall wude be about twelve inches, to what it is up there with nothing underneath 'ee but a mile or two o' fresh air. Fresh air's rare gude stuff to braithe, but' tis mortal poor trade to rest upon, and 'tis a job to raison things out calm and sensible when you zees the houses hanged up in the sky, the sky down 'pon the floor, and the say stood up on end.

After a time Mr. Pilot turned his haid around, and I think he was a bit surprised to vind me still there. But I was hangin' on to me kickin'-strap, don't you make no mistake. When he found he cude'n emp' me out he thought he'd go home. So us come down ; and they lifted me out and stood me on the ground.

And if ever you yers that Jan Stewer have gone flyin' again, you'll know 'tis becus' he've growed wings and turned into a angel.

VI

JAN'S ADVENTURES IN LONDON

I. ON THE UNDERGROUND

DID ever you try to go a journey on that ole Underground Railway, up to Lunnon?

I did once. Never shan't again, I 'ope.

Caw! A feller need to be half a rabbut only to vind his way about in they ole stations. Zac'ly like a rabbut's berry they be. I can't liken 'em to nothin' better. They'm nort but a maze o' tunnels all auver the plaace. Soon's ever you'm out of one tunnel and you thinks now you'm comin' to zomewhere, there's a couple more bevore 'ee, one gwain left-handed and tother gwain right-handed. And don't matter which you takes, you'm sure to be wrong. By the time you've trapesed through half-a-dizzen o' they tunnels you vinds yerzelf back where you started to.

You shude 'a-zee'd the caper I had in that-there ole underground station to Paddyton. Of coorse, 'twas all new to me, and I made about as much haidway as a dog rinnin' around arter his awn tail.

Rissell Square was the place I had to get to, and so-fur as I cude zee I shude a'-bin all-so-well off if I'd wanted to get to Jericho.

The times I rinned up and down they ole tunnels lookin' fer a train! And my ole bags and parcels was like a ton weight.

I wad'n very much better off if I inquired the way of anybody, cus all the volks was coosin' along at sitch a rate I was forced to rin alongzide of 'em while I was spaikin' to 'em; and with my quantity of parcels I wad'n able to keep up the pace long 'nuff to ketch their answer. They was all flyin' along as if they had'n got a minute to live, and time I'd chased after half-a-score of 'em I was pankin' like a sheep and no nearer to findin' me way to Rissell Square than I was when I started.

I determined I'd make the nex' one stap and spaik to me if I had to hang on to his coat-tails. I zee'd a likely lookin' chap comin', so I planked mezelf right bevore 'en.

"Which is the way to Rissell Square, plaise zur?" I said; and I held out me two arms so's he'd be forced to stap and answer me in a proper manner. But the beggerin' toad flipped right out around me and was off again like a long-dog.

However, I heard 'n say, "Change to Piccalilly Circus." And then he disappeared. Down a tunnel.

"Change to Piccalilly Circus!" I says "I wish I cude change to a ferret. Then I shude have a chance to vind me way out o' thase-yer rabbut holes."

I zee'd another chap comin', and I was after 'en, like a cat after a mouse.

"Where's Piccalilly Circus to?"

"You wants Baker Loo," he says, slippin' past me like a strake o' lightnin'.

"Who's he?" I holleyed arter 'en. But he was gone. Down a tunnel.

So I thought to mezelf, "I'll vind ole Baker Loo, whoever he is, and zee what he've got to say about it." So I rished arter the nex' chap I zee'd and shouted to 'en:

"Where shall I vind Baker Loo to, plaise?"

"Down over the staps."

And *he* was gone. Down a tunnel.

"Thank 'ee, sure," I says. "I've bin up and down a vew thousand staps; a hunderd or two more won't make very much odds."

However, I had'n gone very fur bevore I zee'd a big notice up agin the wall, "Bakerloo," and a gurt vinger pokin' out to show 'ee which way to go.

"Us be gettin' on," I says. "I might get there

now bevore I dies of old age, with a bit o' luck."

Presen'ly I come to a gate, and a chap lained up agin' en' with brassen buttons on his coat.

"Ticket," he said to me.

"Thank 'ee, sure," I said, and putt out me hand to take 'n.

"Where's yer ticket to?" he roared at me. Proper nasty about it he was.

"Don't you try to be vunny," I says. "You ab'm give me one, not yet."

Well, and do you knaw, I thought thik feller was gwain to say zummin rude fer a minute. I cude zee the words gwain round and round inzide his faace, but they cude'n vind his mouthe, zeem-zo. Then he had another gude look at me, and I s'pose he zee'd I wad'n properly way-wise, so he tole me I mus' go back and get me ticket to the bookin' orfice.

"That's right," I says. "You zend me back in they ole tunnels again, and I shall be rinnin' around fer the rest o' the wik."

Caw, did'n he laaf? But he took pity on me and showed me where to go and get me ticket to, so I went and got me ticket, and then he knacked a bit out of 'n with a pair o' pinchers, and let me go down on the platvorm.

There was scores and hunderds o' volks stood there waitin', so I putt down me bag and parcels on the vloor to rest a bit. All of a sudden I yer'd a jooce of a roar and a racket, and I zee'd a funny li'l train come up out of a hole.

I cude zee there was gwain to be a bit of a scummer with so many volks all tryin' to get in to-once, so I thought I'd bide back behind a bit and wait till the crush was over. But lo and behold! bevore I had time to look around hardly I'm jiggered if the train wad'n off, and he disappeared into another hole, up tother end.

So I goes up to a porter chap.

" Yer, maister," I says, " thik train id'n gone, is 'er ? "

So he pretended to be lookin' about fer 'n. " Can't zee 'en about no-place," he says.

" But I've got to ride in he," I says.

" You'll have to make 'aste, then," he says. " If you'm dapper enough you mid ketch 'n comin' back."

" Don't none of 'em bide no longer than that?" I says, " Why, down our way they'll wait half-hour zometimes."

" I dersay," he saith. " But l'il places like Lunnun ban't important 'nuff fer that."

With the zame, along comes another train, so this time I made up my mind to squaise in along o' the rest. But my blessid ole parcels tooked up so much rume everybody was pushin' me a-one side, and then I got ketched in the strame o' volks gettin' out o' the train, so the more I tried to go vore the vurder I went back.

However, the porter feller zee'd what was the matter, so he says, "Come on, dad," and he bundled me in, neck 'n crop, haived in my bag and parcels after me, putt fast the door, gived his ole train a shove, and away-to-go with a jit that sent my haid bang up agin the wall.

"If this is trav'lin' in Lunnon," I says, "give me the Muddlecombe carrier's cart."

However, I was een. And my nex' trouble was how was I gwain to get out. I was frightened to death lest I shude go past the place and never know it. I did'n know what the stations was, no more'n a cat, and the train stopped such a short time to each one I had'n got a chance to zee the name aw't. I'd look out o' winder as hard as ever I cude, but all I cude see wude be Oxo, or Navy Cut, or Bass, or Colman's Mustard, or some sitch thing as that.

Every time us come to a station a feller putt his haid in around the door and holleyed out the name aw't. But what he did say I cude'n tell no more'n Adam. It might 'a-bin French or Double Dutch for all I cude make out aw't. Soon's he'd vinished I used to say to the chap nex' to me, "What did 'er zay?" So then he'd repait it to me and I wad'n a bit wiser when he'd said it over again. Half the time I daun' understand what they volks up to Lunnon do say. They zeems to spaik a differnt language, zomehow.

So to-last I said to this-yer feller, "Wude 'ee plaise to tell me when us comes to Piccalilly Circus ?"

" Nex' station," he says.

And the words wad'n hardly out of his mouthe when us flipped into the station and come to a stan'still.

Caw! My dear zaul! 'Twas bad 'nuff gettin' een, but 'twas tain times wiss gettin' out. What a skimpy li'l time they allows 'ee. You zee, I was took on the 'op, as the sayin' is, and I had all the works in the world to gather up my bags and parcels. Everybody's legs zeem to get in my way, and as fast as I picked up one thing I'd let fall two in the place aw't. I was feared of me life I'd be took on to the nex' station. You zee, the trouble was, I wad'n hardly dapper 'nuff to squaise out with the fust party, and time I'd picked up all me belongings and started to go out the new lot was comin' een. So I was in a proper quandairy, sure 'nuff.

And by jo! Soon's the last o' that lot was inzide, the stationmaster was fer shuttin' up the door and shovin' his ole train along. I shouted to 'en:

" Yer," I says, " not so fast. I wants to get out."

"Come on, father," he says, "where have you bin to? Aslape, in under the sate?"

"I ban't your father," I says. "If I had 'a-bin I shude 'a-larned you behaviour."

That's what I said to 'en, and more I shude a-said if I'd had the oppertunity. But he 'oiked me out on the platvorm with my parcels all around me, give a push to his train and away to-go. And when he disappeared in the hole I said:

"Gude-by to 'ee and gude riddance. Nex' time I rides in you I'll walk fer choice."

2. THE RESOLVING STAIRCASE

I vowed I'd never go on the ole underground railway again, arter my fust experience. But I did, s'-know. 'Tis wonderful how soon a body can get accustomed to anything fresh. 'Tis the fust time or two that comes ockerd; and the fust time I went down that ole resolving staircase come darned ockerd to me, I can tell 'ee.

When I told the volks down home about it they did'n hardly know whe'er to believe that there railly was sitch a thing or whe'er 'twas only zome ole yarn I was hatching up. I was tellin' up zome o' my adventures up to Lunnon, and I said:

"One day I went into the underground station

to go a journey and I very zoon lost me way in they ole tunnels and got into a proper bewilderness as usual. So I axed a chap which way to go and he said, 'You wants to go down the resolving staircase.'

"Of coorse, I did'n know what the resolving staircase was like no more'n a dunkey. But I soon vound out.

"They ban't like ordnery stairs. They looks like 'em, fust glimpse. But you daun' have to move yer veet when you'm gwain up-over or down-over. You jis' keep yer veet quite still, and 'tis the stairs which moves up or down, and takes 'ee whichever way you wants to go."

"Yer, stiddy on', Mr. Stewer," says Mrs. Endycott. "What do you take us for, I wonder?"

"Believe it or not, missis," I says; "what I'm tellin' you is gospel. They stairs is all the time on the move."

"I don't zee nothin' very wonderful about that," says Tom Zalter. "I've see'd our stairs, home, do the very same thing. I can mind when the wedding party was, when Jane Tolley's darter was married to Dicky Rew, I got home about o' dree o'clock nex' mornin' and our stairs was gwain round and round and round. Jist like you say, Jan."

"That wad'n my case, Tom Zalter," I said. "I had'n bin to no wedding party, and I had'n had no trouble about gettin' my hat on. And another thing. It wad'n the stairs only in your case, but the furniture and all was gwain around.

" I'm beggered if that id'n true, Jan," he says. " I know 'tis true, cus there was a toad of a chair stood up agin the wall, and every time I went to sit down on the blessid thing he'd flip half-ways around the rume and let me go down on the floor, wop."

" Well, with me," I says, " nothin' else wad'n movin' around excep' the stairs, so the simtims id'n zac'ly. I tell 'ee, thase-yer resolving stairs is alwis on the move ; one lot gwain upperds and tother lot gwain downwerds, accordin' to which way you wants to be took. Wance you've stood 'pon the fust stap you've no call to move yer veet. The same stap that you'm stood upon up to the tap will take 'ee right down to the bottom, and the rest o' the staps is rinnin' along in front or trucklin' along behind. And 'tis a turrable high staircase, too. I shude say 'tis every bit as high as the church tower, and 'twude make ee' proper tired to go up and down in the ordnery fashin."

" What happens to all the stairs when they gets to the bottom, then ? " axed Mrs. Snell.

" I dunnaw what happens to 'em. They disappears out 'o sight in the ground, and where they goes to tho I can't tell 'ee."

"They must use up a mortle lot o' stairs in the coorse of a twelve-month," says Tom.

"They must fer certin'," I says. "But you may depend they've got zome way o' using the zame ones over again."

"And you say you zee'd this with yer awn eyes?" says Mrs. Endycott.

"Zeed it! Laur bless the wumman, don't I tell 'ee I had a ride on the blessed thing. Do 'ee think I draimed it, or what?"

"Bothered if I knows what to think, hardly," her saith.

"I shude be frightened to death," says Mrs. Snell. "Supposin' the whole lot was to go down all to-once instaid o' one to a time?"

"You'd get there all the quicker fer that," says Tom.

"'Tis all right once you'm on," I says, "but 'tis a ticklish job gettin' on the fust time; although 'tis aisy nuff arter you gets in the way aw't. There's a bit of a smooth place rinnin' along on the ground jis' bevore you comes to the stairs, like a rap of the floor moving, and you staps upon that one, and then o' coorse you'm movin' along too. Well, and that carries 'ee vore to the top o' the stairs. Natcher'ly, you ups with yer voot to putt 'n down the fust stap, when lo and behold! you discovers that the other voot which you'm standin' on is one stap down already. And while you'm lookin' at 'n, and wonderin' how the diggins he got there, he'm two staps down. And then dree; and vower; and vive. And when you looks around behind to zee what have happened you vinds you'm a dizzen staps from the top. And you ab'm moved! And by this time you'm two dizzen from the top, and still gwain down.

"And bless yer 'art, if you rest yer bag down 'pon the stap behind 'ee, he'll come down too. Volleys 'ee down wan stap to a time he do, till you gets to the bottom."

"And did you say they'll take 'ee up the zame, Jan?"

"Ees, Tom. Take 'ee up the zame. Once you've got yer voot 'pon the bottom stap you ab'm got to do nothin' more till you vinds yerzelf up top."

"'Tis a very nice way o' doin' it," he says. "I wish us had one like that, home."

"There's jis' one thing I ab'm told 'ee yet," I says, "which id'n quite so nice; or at laiste, it wad'n so nice when I done it. Of coorse, it did'n hap'm after the fust time, but now I've told 'ee half the tale I must tell 'ee tother half. You knows what the chap said when he falled off the church steeple, daun' ee'? He said, ''Tid'n the gwain down what matters very much. 'Tis stoppin' down the bottom.' And that's how 'twas with me on the ole resolving staircase. All the way down I was thinkin' to mezelf, 'I 'ope I shall be able to get off all right,' and when I got nearly to the bottom I zee'd a notice sticked up:

" 'Stap off with the RIGHT voot.'

" Now I knowed in a minute that was wrong, cus I larned all about 'stapping off' when I was in the Special Reserve. 'Twad'n a gurt lot that I did larn, cus my brains wude'n hold it all; but if there was one thing I did remember more'n another 'twas that you must alwis stap off with the LEFT voot. Caw, did'n the ole drill sarjent, and the sarjen-major, and the coloured sarjent, and the captin, and even Colonel Brown hiszelf spend days and wiks tryin' to knack that into my haid. Half the scummers us got into was only becus us wude ferget and go stappin' off with the right voot. 'Twas a wonder us had'n lost the war through it. And what names they did call us.

" 'When fer gudeness' sake be I gwain to larn 'ee alwis to stap off with the left voot?' they use to say. Said it to me, they have, scores and hunderds o' times.

" So I knowed in a minute that notice was all wrong. And I drawed a young feller's attention to it what was stood beside me on the ole resolving staircase.

"You volks up in Lunnon don't know everything, I zee," I said to 'en. "Us country bumkins can larn 'ee zummin arter all. You must never stap off with the right voot. 'Tis all wrong. 'Tis against the rules. You must alwis stap off with the left voot, and if you daun't believe me you can ax Colonel Brown. He ought to know, fer he've bin stappin' off all his life.

"And with the zame us come to the smooth part down the bottom where 'tis rinnin' along the ground, and you've got to stap off on to the platvorm. So I putt across me left voot, and stapped off in a proper manner.

"What happened next I can't tell 'ee, zac'ly. Zummat give me a tremenjis jit, and I thought fer a minute I was flippin' up the stairs again, back'erds. Then I zee'd the station platvorm dap up in the air as if there'd bin a earthquake. The train lines all tied theirzels up in knots, and a hugly gurt weighin' machine took one jump at me and sent me scat along the floor.

"When the volks had stood me the right way up, the young feller said to me:

"'Thank 'ee very much fer showin' me the correc' way. I've never tried it like that, but I will do one o' these days when I be tired o' life.'"

3. JAN AT THE HOTEL

Zeeming to me, when a feller's up in Lunnon his troubles is never over. You'm no zooner out o' one quandairy than you'm into another; and that's the honest truth, begad.

When I was pushed out with the crowd from the lift into the strate, there to the underground station, I stood like a fool frightened. I did'n know which way to go no more 'n a gawk.

However, I'd got the derections of the hotel where I had to go to. The parsen had wrote it all down on a bit of a ticket bevore I left home. He said 'twas a very nice place fer me to go to, and where he alwis went to hiszelf. So I thought if 'twas gude nuff fer a parsen 'twas gude nuff fer me. "Continental Hotel, Rissell Square," that's what was wrote on the ticket, in the parsen's own han'writin'. I cude show it to 'ee now, cus I've got the ticket home.

So I went up to a policeman and I let 'n zee this-yer ticket, and I axed 'n did he know any sitch plaace? 'Tis wonderful what they policemen *do* know, 'pon me zaul. He putt me on the right track in a minute.

"Second turnin' on the left," he said. And I'm jiggered if he wad'n right. Zac'ly right, he was. I turned around the second to the left, and there 'twas, right bevore me. I knowed 'twas the right place drec'ly I ketched sight aw't, cus there was the name up over the door, in letters as long as yer arm: Continental Hotel. 'Twas zac'ly the zame as what the parsen wrote down on the ticket which he let me have bevore I left home. I compared the two, one letter to a time, and 'twas zac'ly right to a vigger.

My dear days, what 'tis to be educative.

But laur bless 'ee, cheel, I was properly frightened to zee the place, I was reely. 'Twas a masters gurt mansion jis' like a king's palace. Whatever do 'em want to erec' sitch tremenjis places for? The squire's houze id'n one-quarter the size, and he've 'most alwis got two or dree rumes stood empty.

"My dear life," I thought to mezelf, "if once I gets properly inzide o' thikky place I shall never get out again. I shall lost mezelf fer certin."

There was half-a-dizzen long stonen staps to go up to the vore door. And what do 'em want sitch gurt doors for? There never wad'n nobody that size, fer certin. And why do 'em want two doors in place o' one? Unless 'tis one to go een and tother to come out.

"However," I thought to mezelf, "they can't ait me, that's a sure thing." So up I goes, up they stonen staps, with me bag in me hand and me parcels in under me arm, and I was jis' 'pon the point of openin' the door; in fact, I'd set down me bag on the staps, and was raichin' vore me hand same purpose to push 'n open, when a feller pulled 'n open from tother zide. Of coorse, I thought he was wantin' to come out, so I dapped back a bit out the way aw'n. But instead of he comin' out, all he done was to start bowin' and scrapin' as if he was gwain to zing a zong, or make up a bit of a recitation. So of coorse, as he was bowin' to me I cude'n do no other than bow to he. And there us bide, like a couple o' jack-in-the-boxes, he bowin' to me and me bowin' to he.

Wull, I putt up with it fer a bit, and then I said, "Be you comin' out or no? Cus if you ban't comin' out I shude like to come een."

But all he said was to go on bowin' like a Punch and Judy show. So I ups with me bag and marches right past 'n. I took 'n to be some sort of a officer chap, with his blue coat and his brassen buttons. But I discovered arterwards he was putt there same purpose to open the door to volks comin' een.

Lunnon's a wonderful place, 'pon me zaul. Jis' you vancy keepin' a chap in brassen buttons to open the door to ole Jan Stewer.

However, I was een ; and I wad'n a lot better off than when I was out, fer what to do ner where to go to I did'n know no more'n a cat. There was heaps o' volks dappin' about one way and another. I know there was, cus they keep on hitchin' their veet in my parcels. But which aw'm belonged to the place and which the place belonged to I cude'n tell fer the life o' me.

However, I reckoned the door-openin' chap wude know zummin about it, so I went up and spoke to he.

" I beg pardon, mister," I says, " but cude you plaise to tell me if there's sitch a thing as a spare bed in the place where I cude sleep to-night ? "

" I cude'n tell 'ee," he saith, " but if you go and spaik to the young lady in the orfice, her know'th all about it."

Well ; to tell 'ee the truth, I wad'n very fast about that. Between you and me and the gate-paust it did'n zeem hardly the sort o' thing to discuss with a young lady you'd never zee'd bevore in yer life. I'd much rather the chap had told me hiszel', but he'd gone back to his bowin' and scrapin'. I did'n zee no other hope fer't, so I went over-cross to the place where the young lady cude look out through the li'l winder, and I wished her " gude-arternune."

Nice, affable maid her was as anyone cude wish vor, and her did'n zeem to mind me spaikin' to her the laistest bit in the world. Her wished me "Gude-arternune" as if us had knowed one-tother fer years.

But all zame fer that, I did'n veel what you might call comferable. Wull, I did'n know how to broach the subjic', if you understand my meanin'. And I'm popped if I did'n make a proper fule of mezelf.

I did! I made a proper fule of mezelf.

What's think I said to thik maid? What *do* you think I said?

"Excuse me, my dear," I said, "but can I bide yer all night?"

Laur, her took me up in a minute.

"You can if you wish," her says. "But wude'n 'ee zooner sit down zometimes?"

I zee'd in a instant what a stoobid remark I'd made, and us had a gude laaf. Both of us did. Her laafed and I laafed too. And arter that us got on like a houze a-vire. 'Tis wonderful what a gude laaf will do towards breakin' the ice, as the sayin' is. You might veel strange with anybody fer a wik, but once you've had a gude laaf together you'm friendly in one minute.

"Did you want a bedrume?" her saith.

"Yes, plaise, my dear, if you've got one to spare. I've brought me own nightshurt, and a brish and comb, and everything I requires. All I wants is a bed fer the night ; and my wife impressed upon me that I was to be sure and ax you if you'd plaise to zee that he'd been properly aired."

So then her laafed again. I dersay her guessed I come up from the country. I'll make a bet her did. Aw! they can tell, bless yer 'art. You mid depend they can tell. But her was very considerate to me all the zame. Her did'n zeem to matter how much trouble her took. Rale nice maid her was ; and I promished her if ever I got back to Deb'mshur alive I'd zend her a pound o' craime. And I did, too. And a whole lot of explanations I had to make to my missis about that there craime, sure nuff.

However, the young lady said her cude spare me a bedrume all right. So then her pushed me out a bit of a doccyment, which her said I must full in.

" What's this," I said, " a dog lishence ? "

" No," her says. " That's fer your nationalality."

" I don't want none," I says. " All I wants is a bed fer the night and a bit o' brexis in the mornin'. I don't want none o' they ole fantastical itums."

Her laafed more'n ever. I s'pause her thought I was a quare ole card.

" Tid'n nothin' to ait," her says. " Everybody must full in one o' they, never mind if he's Archbishop o' Canterbury."

" Well, I ban't he," I says. " You plaise to give me instructions what to putt down, missie, 'cus I ban't very much in the habit o' gwain about to thase places."

" 'Tis nort to do," her says. " Jis' write yer name down there, lookee. Now, what's yer nationalality."

" Wull, I was alwis brought up to the church, and that's where I was baptised to. But I've been to chapel, manys-a-times, although I ban't a methody after that."

Caw! Did'n her laaf ? I shude think her must 'a-bin very glad I come. Her was gettin' plenty of intertainment out aw't, zeem-zo.

" You don't understand. Nationalality is meaning what country you belongs to. What countryman be 'ee ? "

" Deb'm."

" No, no. Deb'm id'n a country."

" Best country in the world," I says ; and purty smart, too. I wad'n gwain to have no Lunnon cockney upholdin' their rows of houses bevore Deb'm.

" Best country in the world," I says, " eether fer mait or drink, or man or maid. Although,"

I says, " it must 'a-bin a middlin' gude country what turned you out."

I thought I'd better-way putt in that li'l bit, becus if her was to turn nasty her cude make it turrable ockerd fer me. But her only laafed. I never zee'd sitch maid to laaf in all my born days.

" I spose if you'm Deb'm you mus' be British," her says.

" My dear cheel," I says. " When you went to skule did'n they larn you no hist'ry? Why, if there had'n bin no Deb'm there never wude'n 'a-bin no British."

" Aw, well," her saith, " you write down British, and you'll be all right."

So I putt down British; though I reckon it shude 'a-bin Deb'm, arter that.

Her opened a gurt buke and rinned her vinger down over the list. Then her wrote down a vigger on a bit of a ticket. I've got 'n home now. I keeps 'n fer what they calls a sheffoneer.

" Rume number vive hunderd and twenty one," her saith.

" Aw, gude laur! Ab'm 'ee got one nearer than that? He sounds a turrable long ways off."

But he wad'n.

Her putt her vinger to one o' they li'l knobs

what rings a bell, and up comes a chap they calls " Butes," becus he wears shoes. He must 'a-come up droo the floor I reckon.

" Vive, two, one."

He ups with my bag, sticks a parcel in under each arm, hanged two or dree around his neck, away-to-go like a long-dog, me after the tail of 'n, daps into the lift, up us goes in the air, out o' the lift, licks along a drangways, flips into a rume, he drops my parcels, " Vive, two, one," and then he disappeared back droo the floor where he come from.

4. THE EVER OPENING DOOR

If I was to bide very long up there to Lunnon I sh'd go mazed. I know I shude. I sh'd go mazed, with so much ole hurry-skurry and turmoil, so much uproar and bewilderness, and so much gettin' out of other people's way.

Caw! My dear life, you'm on the hop-skip-an'-jump from mornin' to night. They thinks you can't be injoyin' yerzelf without you'm trapesin about, yer, there and everywhere. But I'd rather take things a bit more leisurable. Zeeming to me the volks up to Lunnon is never content with what they'm on-upon now; they mus' be all the time fidgettin' about what they'm gwain to do next. They don't appear to take no delight in sittin' down quiet and comferable fer half-hour and just thinking. All they delights in is to be flippin' about from one ole kickshaw to another like a passel o' grasshoppers.

And what hours they do keep to be sure. They never zeems to think about gwain to bed till purt' near time to get up. They can't get no buty sleep fer certin; and most aw'm wants it bad nuff, gudeness knows.

Wad'n I zome tired when I went to bed the fust night in that hotel. I cude scarcely drag one voot behind the tother. I can zee now why they wants they ole lifts about so much. When it comes end o' the day they ab'm sufficient sproil left to climb up over stairs to go to bed, so they've got to be hoisted up like a sack o' grain gwain into the mill.

When I waked up nex' mornin' and opened me eyes, do you think I cude make out where I was to? I cude'n tell no more than nothing. I gappied all around the rume, but I'm bothered if I cude size it up at all. Everything was strange, and I beginned to wonder whether I had'n bin carr'd off by the pixies or no. There wad'n nuff light in the rume to zee very well, and I thought I'd waked up in the middle o' the night. So I tooked out my watch from in under the piller, and 'twas upright zeb'm by that one.

I knawed that cude'n be right cus 'twas too dark. Then I thought praps I fergot to wind 'n up the night bevore and this was yesterday's time. But I cude yer 'n ticky, so it cude'n be that. So I said to mezelf, " I'll go and look out o' winder and zee if I can vind out what *have* happened."

I cude distinc' the winder all right. Looked like's if 'twas munelight. The blind was down, so I putt me hand to the tossel, thinkin' I was gwain to pull 'n up, when all of a sudden I got sitch a start, I purt' near jumped out o' me skeen. The blind flied up out o' me vingers like a bow-'n-arrow, bang up to the top o' the winder; and with the zame, in come the zin shining nuff to scorch anybody's eyes out. Thik ole blind was black and thick, but the instant he was out the way the whole place was a blaze of light.

" Gude heavens above! " I says, " 'tis zeb'm o'clock all right, and no cows fetched in, no hosses attended to, no poultry fed, no calves' milk on, no nort. Half the mornin' gone and nothin' done and me lied in bed."

Then o' cou'se it all come back to me, and I remembered there wad'n no cows ner pigs to zee to. But how ever I come to sleep on till that hour I cude'n think. 'Twas pokin' about to such a redecklus time the night bevore ; that's what done it.

And of coorse, through me not bein' way-wise in regards to hotels I wasted ever so much time over gettin' mezelf dressed. For one thing I wanted to wash, but there wad'n a jug o' watter and a basin, as I thought there wude 'a-bin. I wude'n 'a-mattered that a bit if I'd knowed where the pump was to. I'd all-so-soon have washed in under the pump as any place else, but I had'n the laistest idaya where to go fer 't. And where was I to get hot watter to shavee? I tell 'ee straight, I beginned to wish I was back along o' mother, where I cude holley down over stairs fer whatever I wanted. Made me veel most mortal lonesome. All that granjer and I cude'n have a wash. Plenty of pomp and no pump, as you might say.

Jist then I zee'd a sort of a basin sticked up agin the wall. Natcher'ly, I'd bin lookin' fer a basin with a jug stood up inzide, but this one had two taps pokin' out from the wall. I turned on one o' the taps to zee if any watter wude come, and if I did'n give a shout, then I'm a

Dutchman. The watter was scaal-hot, min, and I had me hand in under the tap. Made me hop around, I can tell 'ee. And when I come to look I zee'd the word "Hot" 'pon-top the tap; and I knowed it was the truth. There was no need to putt "Hot" on it, begad. You cude veel that for yerzelf. Jis' you vancy havin' boilin' hot watter inzide anybody's bedrume only by turnin' on a tap. But very convaynient, mind, cus I was abble to shavee and everything.

But what with one ole hinedrance and another 'twas upright eight bevore I went downstairs to get me brekfas'. I was ashamed to look anybody in the faace, and I did'n expect no other but what all the grub wude be ait, and none left fer me. I zee'd my ole friend the "Butes," so I axed 'n if all the brekfas' was done away.

"Done?" he says. "Why, 'tis only eight o'clock."

"Only eight!" I says. "What time do the volks up yer go to work for gudeness' sake?"

He did'n zeem to know what to make o' that so I axed which was the way to the kitchen.

"What do you want the kitchen for?" he says.

"For me brekfas' of coorse. Did 'ee think I wanted to have me hair cut?"

"Brekfas' rume straight in through on the right."

I wad'n aware there was a proper rume fer brekfases, so I told 'n I was quite willin' to have it in the kitchen if 'twude save any work or bother clearin' up. But he did'n zeem to jump at it, I did'n fancy; so I went on to where he said, and I thought to mezelf, "If they mind fer me to bissle up their best parler 'tis their own look-out."

And then I had another ole scare, which done me out of zeb'm year's growth. 'Pon me word, when you come to consider the number of times I was frightened out of me wits 'tis a wonder I ever come back alive to tell the tale. I got as fur as the double doors o' the brekfas' place and reached vore my hand to turn the hannle when the doors started to open, bevore I cude touch 'n.

Of coorse, I thought there mus' be zomebody comin' out, and yet 'twas strange, cus all the top half of the doors was glass so I shude 'a-bin able to view anybody on the inzide. However, I considered it must be zome li'l short body, or else a cheel, so I dapped back out the way to let 'em pass.

But nobody come out, and the doors shut fast again.

"That's funny," I said to mezelf. "Zomebody must have opened the doors fer certin, and twad'n me, cus I never titched 'n."

So I goes vore again to push the door open, and I'm popped if the zame thing did'n hap'm again. Bevore I cude reach my hand to the hannle the doors opened. And there wad'n nobody there. I knowed there wad'n, cus I stood fast where I was and I cude view the whole thing right in through. And there wad'n nobody there. Not a zaul.

At laiste, there wad'n nobody visible to the naked eye; but I tell 'ee straight I beginned to wonder whe'er there wad'n a ghost in the place or no. However, there was no sainse in me stood there lookin' so I went in through, and I was no sooner inzide than the darned ole doors shut theirzels. Or else a ghost shut 'em.

But what a grand place 'twas in there. Tell about gwain in the kitchen! Anybody wude think they was expectin' the Laurd Mayor o' Lunnon. There was scores o' tables about all over the place, all to a glitter like a jew'ler's shop winder, but only about half-a-dizzen was occupied.

" This mus' be the last lot jus' finishin' up," I thought to mezelf. But I found out arterwards 'twas only the fust lot jis startin'. When I'd finished and was gwain out the rest was jus' thinkin' about comin' een.

And if you'll believe me, when I got up to they blimmin' doors, if they did'n carry on the zame caper again. Soon's ever I got close up they started to open. Never titched 'em, I did'n, and never said a word to 'em. They opened o' their own accord.

" Whatever's come over the blessid doors ? " I said. " Have 'em got eyes ? Can they zee me comin' ? "

Mind, I wad'n aware I'd said it out loud. But I spause I must a-done zo, cus a gen'lman behind me started laafin'.

" 'Tis a patent," he says. " When you putts yer weight on the mat it makes the doors open."

And I'm beggered if it wad'n true, too ; cus I tried it ever so many times to prove it. Drec'ly I putt me voot on the mat they doors beginned to open ; and soon's ever I stapped back they shut to again. How 'tis done I can't tell 'ee ; and I never shude'n 'a-believed it if I had'n witnessed it with my awn eyes.

Well, well ? 'Tis same's I've said bevore ;

they'm wonderful volks up to Lunnon fer savin' theirzels work. But jis' you fancy wantin' a patent to open the door for 'em. I suppose the nex' thing they'll have is a machine to blow their noses.'

Chapter VII

A MAN OF INVENTION

JOE CLAMPITT was a master-card for inventions. Absolutely full of inventions, Joe Clampitt was. He cude scheme out inventions fer anything you like to putt bevore 'n. Tell 'n what you wanted done, and in two minutes he'd explain the sort of invention to do it.

Joe Clampitt alwis wude have it to be that there's an invention to do any job on the face of the earth, if you only knowed how to go to work to vind it. There wad'n a scrap o' need, so he said, fer anybody to go toilin' and swattin' and pushin' and haivin' to do any pa'ticler job; cus if you cude only get the right idaya you cude make an invention which wude do all the work as aisy as turnin' yer hand upzide down. And zome'ow or 'nother Joe zeemed to be alwis able to get the idayas.

"I dunnaw mezelf how I do's it," he says. "'Tis a gift, I suppose, jis' like zome people has the gift o' vindin' watter with a hazel twig.

They can't explain what makes the twig twist around when they passes over watter, and I can't explain what makes the idayas come into me haid when I sees a job that wants doin'. But the instant I sees what it is that have got to be done I can picsher the right invention to do it."

And Joe wude not only picsher it, but if you let 'n have a vew carpenter's tools and a rap or two of board and a long length of wire and heaps o' nails and plenty o' rume to make a mess he'd construct it for 'ee, pervided you cude wait long enough.

Scores of inventions Joe have made fer different people around the neighbourhood, one time and 'nother, fer savin' time and labour. I'll make a bet you cude'n visit a zingle varm in the parish without vindin' wan or two of Joe's inventions knockin' about, with nothin' the matter with 'em excep' that they won't work.

And that was the only fault with Joe's contraptions. They'd got the idaya all right, and they looked all right, and they'd stand up by theirzel's and all that. The only trouble was they wude'n work.

There was zome people of coorse who tried to make out 'twas all jue to idleness on Joe's part. Whether that was the case or no id'n fer me to say, but I do knaw one thing, he spent a lot more energy and tooked a sight more time over makin' his inventions than what he wude 'a-done if he'd started on the job itzelf in the fust place and done it in the ordnery way. But he was like a gude many else, willin' to do a lot more work if you called it by zome other name. 'Tis wonderful the amount of exertion zome volks will go to as long as they thinks they'm doin' it fer pleasure.

The one who used to suffer most from Joe's benefits, back along, was his wive. The fust week they was married Joe had so many idayas come in his haid fer inventions to save labour, he'd have had the brain-faver if it had'n been fer one thing. Within a vortnit he'd cut off the dog's haid and the cat's tail with an invention fer choppin' sticks; broke zeb'm sheets o' glass with a patent fer clainin' winders; pushed a hole in the ceilin' with a contraption fer doing its own white-washin'; and smashed up I dunnaw how many plates and dishes with an invention fer ketchin' mice. But Mrs. Clampitt bein' newly married putt that all down to the contryness of the inventions, not to any fault of Joe's. 'Twad'n till he trigged up his patent fer workin' the mangle that her beginned to have her doubts. The very fus' time her axed 'n to turn the mangle for her Joe turned the hannle round about o' twice, and that was nuff!

"I knows a better way than that," he says. "You go and vind another job fer a bit. I shall fix up an invention to do this one."

Mrs. Clampitt was young and innocent in they days, so her went off and left Joe to fix up his invention. What he done I can't tell 'ee zac'ly, but I knaw he made fast a barreel to the wheel o' the mangle, and had a long rope and winded around the barreel. He knacked a couple o' bricks out o' the wall o' the wash-houze and pushed out the end of the rope through this-yer hole into the garden. Then he had in the hoss. The idaya was to harness the hoss to this-yer rope and make 'n walk down the garden path away from the wash-houze, and this wude natcher'ly twest the barreel around and so turn the mangle.

When his invention was all ready to work Joe called to his missis. Her was frightened when her went in and zee'd the hole in the wash-houze wall; spesh'ly as Joe had'n bin too pa'ticler as regards to makin' up a sture, and the dist and the grit and bits o' morter had gone all over missis's clane washin'. As I said bevore her had'n bin married to 'en very long so her did'n say the things to 'en that her wude 'a-done later on. Joe told his wive to putt all the biggest and hardest things her'd got in the mangle and he'd show her how to get the work over quick.

'Twas all the wonders in the world that the poor li'l wumman had'n bin killed outright. How her wad'n I dunnaw. Her putt in a gurt sheet in the mangle and then her holleyed to Joe through the hole in the wall to say her was ready. That was her instructions from Joe. But he, the gurt gawk, anxious to try his patent, and a bit excited I s'pause, instead o' waitin' a second fer his wive to get back to the mangle, as soon as her said " Ready," he give the hoss a gude strip with a stick. The hoss purt' near jumped droo his coller and away-to-go like a shot from a gun. The rope on the barreel did'n unwind like it was ordained to, but it slipped off one end and got hitched up ; so the hoss pulled the rope and the rope pulled the mangle right across the wash-houze. 'Twas a mercy Mrs. Clampitt wad'n ketched in between the mangle and the wall. Her only jumped away jist in the nick o' time, and even then the corner of the mangle fetched her sitch a scat on the arm her wad'n able to raise her hand to her haid fer a week.

Joe was makin' so much noise of his own outzide that he cude'n yer the racket gwain on in the wash-houze, and so the ole mangle went coosin' across the floor, smashin' up the washing tubs and the stool and clothes baskets and the buckets, till it come to the wall and cude'n go no further. Joe went inzide to see what was the matter. What he cude'n see fer hiszelf his wive pointed out to 'en. It was the moment, you might say, when their honeymune finished, and Mrs. Clampitt feeled that the time had come when her cude spake to her husband as a husband shude be spoke to.

You'd 'a-thought that wude cure Joe of his inventions, but you might as well try to cure the cat of chasing mice. The next one that moves he'll be after 'en again, and the next job of work that Joe had bevore 'n wude call fer another invention. He made a lovely invention to prevent his missis from havin' to go out nights to shut up the ducks. He happened to be there wan night and watch her gwain out when 'twas rainin' heavens hard.

"Us won't have no more o' that," he says. "I'll make a patent to do that job."

So the nex' day he had a long board, long 'nuff to cover all the li'l doors into the ducks' houzes. In the daytime this board was hitched up so's the ducks cude go in and out. But there was a lot o' wires and li'l wheels and things, and one wire went right up over and in droo the back kitchen winder and around a nail in the wall. All you had to do to shut up the ducks of a night was to unhitch the wire off the nail and let it go, and down wude go the board, and the ducks was all shut up. Lucky fer Joe it happened to be a turrable night that night—rainin' and blawin' and dark's a bag.

"See what my patent saves 'ee," he said to his wive; "gwain out a night like this." And her admitted 'twas nice not to have to.

"You'll be able to do it yerzelf in future, lookee. Simply unhook the wire off the nail, let 'n go, and down comes the board."

There's no doubt but what the board come down all right, cus missis found it down the nex' mornin', and vive ducks with their haids in under, all daid as door nails. So another invention went scat.

That was the worst thing about Joe's inventions; they was alwis done fer the gude of other people. If he'd only done 'em all fer his own benevit 'twude 'a-bin all right, cus then he'd 'a-bin the only one to suffer.

Like when Varmer Way grummled cus volks wude leave the gate open in Church Close.

"They've got the benevit of walkin' across my meadow," he says, "instead o' gwain all around the road, and yet they ab'm got the common dacency to hapse the gate behind 'em; and then I gets into trouble becus the cattle goes to road."

"What you wants there, maister," says Joe, "is a patent. I'll make 'ee one. They won't be able to lef' the gate open then, cus he'll close by hiszelf."

Maister did'n mistrust nothing, and nex' day Joe was down to the gate fer sevver'l howers friggin' about with li'l wheels and long wires and heavy weights. I dunnaw what he done, exac'ly, but when you opened the gate the wires across the bottom rinned around the wheels and hauled up the weights in zome way, and then when you let go to the gate the heavy weights did pull it fast again. I never zee'd it in workin' order mezelf, but I s'pause Joe must have got it to his satisfaction bevore he left it. The only trouble was that you had to take care to stap over the wires down bottom; but Joe reckoned the volks wude zoon get used to that.

However, as bad luck wude have it, Varmer Way was up to the Black Oss that night, and havin' sold a cow and calve that mornin' in the market fer twenty-vive pound which he wude willin'ly have took nineteen vor before the oction, he had one or two more than usual. And gwain home along in the pitch dark he went to go droo the gate not knowin' aught about Joe's patent, and he hitched his voot in the wire, and down he goes. Well, then, of coorse, he went potin' about to try and free hiszelf, but instead o' that he got both veet tangled up in such a fashin that he cude'n rise, and the more he went kickin' about the more he got cot up in the wire. And every time he pushed the gate away 'twude come back and give'n a scat in the haid.

Of coorse he roared like a buel, but he might vire off a cannon all out there that time o' night without attractin' anybody's notice. He was there till long arter midnight like a rabbut in a trap, and there he wude have remained till the nex' mornin' if the policeman had'n happened to come along and free 'en.

Varmer went straight home and got his gun and went up to Joe Clampitt's cottage. And he made Joe come out jist as he was, all in the dead waste and middle o' the night, and go down and take all that contraption off his gate. He said he shoot 'n if he did'n, and in the mood varmer was then I wude'n say he wude'n 'a-done it, nuther. Purt' near give Joe his death o' cold, pokin' about there in the dark fer two howers in the draaftiest spot in the parish and nothin' on but his nightshurt.

But the patent which very nearly finished Joe Clampitt was the one he invented last tettie-digging. What Joe ordained doin' was to bag up his etties as he digged 'um and putt 'em up in a loft. The trouble was, the only way up to the loft was a rough sort of ole ladder which wad'n very safe the best o' times, and impossible to carry up a bag o' tetties. But that did'n worry Joe.

"This is jus' where you wants a patent," he says, "and I've got the very idaya."

So what he done, he had the longest oaken board he cude get and trigged up a sort of a say-saw like the chillern goes riding up and down upon, only he had the middle part up as high as possible so that when one end o' the board was down 'pon the ground the other end was right up level to the door o' the loft.

You zee what Joe's plan was. If he putt a load o' tetties on the bottom end o' the say-saw and then weighted down the other end, the tetties wude rise up level to the loft, and all that was necessary was for zomebody to be up there to pull 'em off the board in on to the floor. Joe reckoned his missis wude be able to manage that much. P'raps you thinks, "Why wad'n he up there to do it hiszelf?" But that's where the patent come in. In fact, you might say that Joe *was* the patent. Anyrate, he was the cause that made the patent work, becus he was to be the weight.

Joe explained it all to his wive, bevorehand, and he was some proud of his patent, I can assure 'ee. And so was her, too, come to that, cus it railly did look like as if this one was bound to work proper.

"You can zee fer yerzelf what's gwain to hap'm," he says, "cus us can make it work by hand without puttin' on any weights. This end will rest on the ground to start with, and I shall putt on a bag o' tetties, and that contraption like a sort of a wire cage is to keep the bag in his place when he goes up in the air. When the weight o' the tetties is on one end, of coorse the other end will be pokin' right up—like that. Now, they li'l raps nailed across the board is to allow me to clim' up to the other end. So you zee how 'tis gwain to work. 'Tis eight score bags o' tetties; that's one hunderd and zixty pound, and I weighs eight score and a half. So when I clim's up to the top o' the plank 'twill *just* overbalance, my end will go down nice and gentle and the tetties will go up like that, zee!"

Joe putt his hand to the say-saw and showed her how tother end wude go up in the air.

"There, lookee-zee?" he saith. "The end o' the board comes right on the level o' the door, and not a ninch away. I reckon I've a'justed that butiful. All you'll have to do is to be up there to the door and when the tetties comes up jis' topple the bags off the board on to the floor and then I'll flip up and pack 'em back in their place. I've got twenty bags to go up, and with this patent I reckon it won't be no more than puttin' pots o' jam up top the dresser. Now you dap up the ladder and I'll send 'ee up the fust load."

So missis went up in the loft and stood in the door ready fer the fust bag when it arrived. Joe lifted the bag on to the bottom end o' the say-saw.

"Be 'ee ready, mother?"

"Ees. I'm ready."

"Right! Then I'll jis' clim' up the board and you pull off the bag when he comes up."

So he started scraalin' up the board on his hands and knees. But 'twad'n half so aisy as what he thought 'twas gwain to be. When he got past the half-way the ole board beginned to get shaky and wommle zide-ways a bit; and the furder he went the more he wommled. He had to grip as hard as ever he cude to keep from fallin' off. And he wad'n no-ways near the top, 'eet. He zeemed to be gwain up a turrable heighth, a lot higher than it looked on the ground. The little raps o' wude across the board hurted his knees most jewsive. By the time he got nearly to the top he was frightened to death, cus the ole board was rockin' about to such extent he cude hardly bide on there; and to-last he lied down flat on his chest and let one leg hang each zide. That made 'n veel a bit more safer, but 'twas slower work climmin' up.

However, after a lot of puffin' and blowin' he came to the spot where he beginned to balance.

"Look out, mother; I'm off!"

And he was very nearly. He started ridin' downwards and 'twas all right the fust half o' the journey, cus that brought 'n more level, but after that he started gwain haid fust. Joe had'n thought o' that. 'Twas a hawful sensation. He zeem to be turnin' right upzide down, and he was forced to putt his arms and legs around the ole say-saw and grip tight to keep from slippin' off haidlong. Of coorse, the consequence was, his knees and his elbows and the top of his haid reached the ground, when his end o' board was up a gude six inches; and allowin' fer the bendin' of the board in addition to that, the bag o' tetties did'n reach the level o' the floor not by a voot. And to make matter wiss the ole say-saw had swayed outwards a bit so Mrs. Clampitt had to stretch to reach the bag. It stands to raison her cude'n lift up eight score like that.

But poor ole Joe he wad'n in a position to see what had railly happened, cus in the first place he was the wrong way around, and in the second place he was the wrong end up. Furthermore, his face was down to the ground and he cude'n shift it. But he holleyed all the things he cude think of to his wive to make her hurry up and lift off the load; and her, poor zaul, might jist as well try to pull up a oak tree by the mores.

"Take off the bag I tell 'ee. I can't hang on yer another minute."

Her made one gurt effort to haul up the bag, and anybody must guess what the result wude be. Instead of the bag comin' up her over-balanced and went down. Natcher'ly, her hanged on to the tetties, so down goes that end of the say-saw, and bevore Joe knawed what had happened he shot up in the air like a rocket. If he had'n had hold to the board with his arms and legs he must 'a-went off like a burd flying when his missis reached the ground with a wop. And I won't say but what 'twude 'a-bin the best thing fer 'n; cus when Mrs. Clampitt went down bump her rolled off the say-saw and took the bag o' tetties along with her. Of coorse, when Joe got up to the top there wad'n nothin' to keep 'n there, cus all the weight was gone from tother end. So the only thing fer he to do was to turn around and come down again, which he did, bang, wollop! 'Twas the quickest journey there and back that Joe ever done in his life; or anybody else, fer that matter. Forch'nitly, Mrs. Clampitt wad'n hurted nothin' to spaik of, so her was able to attend to Joe, and he tooked a bit of attendin' to, begad. Luckily he come down haid fust, so nothin' wad'n broke, but 'twas howers bevore he properly got back the li'l bit of sainse which he had to start with. However, it knocked the rest o' the patents out of his haid and Mrs. Clampitt said it was worth being shook about a bit only for that.

VIII

THE LIGHTNING STRIKE

DIFFER'NT people wude have gived 'ee differ'nt reasons why Dan'l Partridge went to Brattery Manor every mornin' and bide there all day.

Dan'l hiszelf wude have told 'ee he went there becus he worked fer Squire Brattery. Squire reckoned he went there to work, which is a differ'nt thing to working there. Mrs. Brattery considered he was a charitable ins'ichution to which her suscribed fer the sake of his wive and chillern. James Barrett, the haid gardener, said he was there to spoil the fruits of other folks's labours, but if he only moved a bit quicker he'd 'a-bin handy to scare away the burds; and 'Lisbeth Partridge, Dan'l's wive, said 'twas a Godsend to get 'n out the way between meals.

Be that as it may, Dan'l went to Brattery Manor every day in the employ of the squire, and drayed his thirty-two and zixpence every week, whether 'twas fer gude, bad, or indifference. Supposed to assist about the gardens he was, and he was termed " odd man." The haid gardener reckoned he was " odd man out." Out o' zight when he was wanted and out o' place when he wad'n.

However, Squire Brattery employed 'n becus nobody else wude'n; or I shude say, Mrs. Brattery did. 'Twas her doin's, railly, 'cus Lisbeth Partridge was the hardest-workin' and most deservin' wumman in the parish, and there was best part of half a score mouths to fill at home.

So Dan'l tooked the edge off the tools and broked abroad the glass in the greenhouses, and by that means he gived employment to two more chaps; which shows that everybody is of some use in the world.

Like most people what ab'm got sufficient gumtion to look arter their own affairs, Dan'l was a gurt chap fer mindin' other volks's business. He use to raid the newspaper rigler every day while he was about his work. There's not many people can raid and work at the zame time, but Dan'l cude manage it aisy. In fac', James Barrett preferred it that way, cus he said that was the only time Dan'l did'n do more harm than gude.

Through the means of Dan'l raidin' the paper so much there wad'n a subjic' he cude'n talk about. Or what I ought to zay, there wad'n a subjic' he *did'n* talk about, which zome volks is ap' to mistake fer the zame thing, whereas 'tis very differ'nt. And that's how he come to be took up with this-yer ole Strike tomfulishness. He'd stidded and pondered the peerations of a parcel of chaps what wude sooner talk than work, and fulled up his haid with 'em to such extaint, that to-last, he come to consider he cude make a spaich with the best of 'em.

And you'll alwis notice that when a feller thinks he *can* make a spaich he reckons he *ought* to make a spaich, never mind whether 'tis worth the makin', and never mind whether anybody wishes to yer it or no.

Wull, one mornin' Dan'l resayved orders to hoe a rap o' turmits. He carr'd on to his job fer a bit, 'genst his backbone beginned to craikee, and then he had a straightener to zee how much he'd done and how much more was left to doing. And when he zee'd what a long row 'twas, and nineteen more such rows arter he'd vinished this one, his 'art went right down in his butes, and he come all over to a cold swat. 'Cus you zee, hoein' turmits is differ'nt to zome jobs. 'Tis fiddlin' work thinnin' out the li'l toads, and anybody can see at a glimpse how much more is left ahaid. Dan'l had got his mind full o' this-yer ole strike mazeness, and when he rinned his eye all over thik expanse of turmits he thought 'twas time he done zummin in the matter.

It so happened that the Squire and Mrs. Brattery and the haid gardener was all away to the flower shaw, so cude'n 'a-bin a better oppertunity. Dan'l stood up top of a weel-barra and made a spaich. He did'n have a very big crowd to spaichify to. There was Jim Cole the stable chap and Alfy Steer the houze-boye, Fred Discombe the under gardener and Jinny Mudge the kitchen-maid. But Dan'l considered that was plenty to start a strike with, cus the rest wude be only too ready to join een when they zee'd how they was gwain to benevit. So he off with his 'at, drowed out one arm and started.

"Ladies an' gen'lmen."

"That won't do, Dan'l," says Jim. "There's only Jinny yer, and you can't make more'n one lady out of her; and I doubt very much if you cude do that."

"I shude like to know where he gets his gen'lmen to," says Jinny. "I don't zee none."

"Hold thee baal," says Dan'l. "This is gwain to be a proper spaich, and every proper spaich starts with 'Ladies and Gen'lmen,' whether there's any there or no. You ab'm got to interfere; only harken to what I do say and putt in 'Yer, yer,' when I do say aught prominent."

"Right you be, Dan'l," says Jim. "Get on with the prominents."

"The time have come, my brither workers," says Dan'l, "when us have got to stand up fer our rights, one and all, young and old. Us have bin trod underfoot long enough. Us be nort else but worms. That's what us be, worms. You'm a worm Jim Cole, and Alfy Steer is nort but a worm, and——"

"Yer, stiddy on ol' man," says Jim. "Not quite so much o' yer worms. If you goes terming me a worm I'll give thee a clump 'long-zide the yerawl, and quick about it."

This putt Dan'l off his stroke a bit, 'cus Jim's a hefty gurt chap, and a bit of a vightin' feller.

"You misunderstan's my meanin'," he says, in a differ'nt sort o' voice. "When I says you'm a worm, that's only in a manner o' spaikin'."

"Wull, I don't like yer manner o' spaikin'," says Jim. "You can call the boye a worm if you like, 'cus he looks a bit like a worm. But you can't call it to me, so I warn 'ee."

"Why shude I be called a worm, any more 'n you?" says the boye. But Jim give 'n a tack in the yer, and told 'n not to interfere with the spaich; and Dan'l said if he did'n stap yaalin' he wude'n be 'lowed to join the union.

"What my meanin' is, is this," says Dan'l. "Us ab'm got no rights. Everybody is intitled to his rights. This is supposed to be a free country, and why shude one have everything and tother have nort? Why shude Squire Brattery be rollin' about on a bed of golden suvrins, and you and me be slavin' and toilin' in the swat of our brow?"

"When did you swat last?" says Fred.

"Last time he zee'd a job o' work," says Jim.

"Yer, yer," says the boye; and Dan'l promished 'n a gude larrupin' if he did'n bide quiet, cus he was afeared to tackle eether o' the chaps.

"You said I had to say, 'Yer, yer,' when anything prominent was said," says Alfy, "and I reckon that was prominent."

"You spaik when you'm axed to spaik," says Dan'l. "There's a sight too much class-hatred in the land, and that's what's the matter. The rich is up 'pon-tap, and the poor is down under, and 'tis time 'twas altered. Where wude the bosses be to, if 'twad'n fer they what do's the work? That's what I wants to knaw! And there's another thing I wants to knaw. Why shude one body be able to drive about in his carriage and another have to theen out a lot o' bais'ly ole turmits? Tell me that. And tell me this, likewise. What do Squire Brattery do fer his livin'? Nort! And what do he get fer doin' it? Thousands o' pounds a year. And what do I do? Workin' and toilin' and moilin' from dayslight to dark night."

"Yer, yer," says all the lot of 'm, but Dan'l did'n zim to be plaised altogether with the way they said it.

"And what do I get fer it?"

"I knaws what you ought to get fer it," says Jim. But Dan'l did'n stap to yer what 'twas. He went on with his narration bevore Jim had time to finish.

"Look at you, Jim Cole. Look at the howers you've got to work and slave. And what do you get? A miserly vive and thirty shullins a week."

"And me lodge free, Dan'l. Muzzen ferget to chuck that een."

"Lodge! Hang about lodge! What do that cost 'em? There's the rumes there, and bin there fer ginerations, and if you wad'n occupyin' 'em they'd lie idle, wude'n 'um? That id'n money, is it? If you was starvin' hungerd cude you take one o' they rumes to the shop and buy a loaf o' braid wai't?"

"And all me meals every day, Dan'l. Muzzen laive they out."

"Meals be blawed! What's a vew meals to they? What do 'um send out to you? Only what they daun' want on their own table, same's they wude to the doug. That's all you be, Jim Cole——"

He was gwain to say "a doug," but he ketched Jim's eye in time, so he finished up with, "traited like a doug. That's what you be."

"And the milk, Dan'l. Everybody gets allowance of milk, as much as they can do wai'."

"Milk, Jim Cole! What's that fer gudeness sake? What they putts out fer the cat."

"Aw, be I cat as well? Worm, doug, cat. You mid-so-well make it minagerie and finish wai't."

"Wull, that only shows 'ee where us have got ground down to. 'Long o' the beasts o' the vield. But the time have come to rise. Us mus' strike fer dree pound a week, and not one penny less. Remember, the idle rich is in our hands. They can't do nothin' wai'out we. Be you prepared to stan' up fer yer rights or no?"

"You show us how 'tis done, Dan'l," says Fred. "Us ban't so book-larnid as what you be."

"I'll be the laider," says Dan'l, "and you've only got to do what I tells 'ee. All us wants is a lightnin' strike. Us'll down tools this very minute and refuse to do a thing fer 'em till they pays us dree pound a week. They'll be back very shortly, and when they vinds there id'n gwain to be nothin' done they'll be on their hands and knees. I give 'em twenty-vower hours. By that time they'll zee that us be the rale masters ; and when you'm drayin' yer dree pound a week, you'll say, 'See what Dan'l Partridge have done fer me.' The end of oppression have come. Us mus' spread the wings of independence and fly up in the face of tyrannical injistice."

Dan'l had larned that bit out o' the paper and he'd bin savin' it up to make a grand finish. But unforchnitly, he drowed up his arms so much he upzot the weel-barra and went back'erds tap-over-tail into a cowcumber frame.

" You did'n spread yer wings hardly quick nuff, Dan'l," says Jim.

" Never mind, us'll spread 'em now," he says. " The order is, down tools fer dree pound a week."

When James Barrett returned he vound Dan'l lained up agin a paust with his han's in his pockets.

" Ab'm you finished they turmits 'eet, Partridge ? "

" Ab'm you got no eyes in yer haid ? Can't you zee I be on strike ? Us be all on strike, and there id'n gwain to be no more work done on this plaace till us gets dree pound a week apiece. So you can tell that to the squire, and when you wants me back upon proper terms you'll vind me to the Ring o' Bells."

As a matter o' fac', the haid gardener did'n say a word to nobody 'cus to tell the truth he was glad nuff to have Dan'l out the way. But bim-bye the squire and his lady strolled around the gardens and Mr. Barrett told 'em this li'l ditty. Squire laafed fit to bust hiszelf and said James was to look out fer zomebody else in the place aw'n.

But Mrs. Brattery is a bit mooty-'arted and her thought ov Lisbeth Partridge drec'ly.

"Her's a hard-workin' wumman," her says, "but what's her gwain to do with all they chillern and nothin' comin' in from Partridge. You laive him to me. I'll zee if I can't larn him a lesson."

Her went straight down to Dan'l's cottage and had a chat with Lisbeth Partridge. What transpired I can't tell 'ee, but I reckon Dan'l's yers shude 'a-scorched his hat. It took my lady a long time persuadin' Mrs. Partridge, but her got her in the mind aw't to-last.

Presen'ly Dan'l, down to the Ring o' Bells, had a sort of a veelin' that 'twas zupper-time, so he pegged away home. He had a wonderful gude wive, Dan'l had, and 'twas amazin' the meals her used to cook fer'n, considerin' what li'l time her had and the small amount o' money comin' een. But o' cou'se, her use to carr' back lots o' li'l things that was give to her to the places where her went to work. So Dan'l was lookin' vorrad to zummin tasty as usual.

You can imagine what he veeled like when he got home and vound the table all bare, and his wive sot down raidin' the newspaper.

"Where's my zupper to?" he says.

"I dunnaw nothin' about yer zupper. I'm on strike."

"You'm what!"

"On strike, zame's the rest o' the volks. Why shude I go on workin' and slavin' fer the vew paltry shullins you takes home every week? I never gets a rest ner a 'olladay like zome women, and I ban't gwain on like it no more till you pays me dree pound a week."

"How can I pay 'ee dree pound a week, stoobid?"

"Wull, there! That's your look out."

Dan'l was properly strick dummy. He turned around and went back to the Ring o' Bells to 'low her to come to her sainses. By the time he got home, last thing o' night, his stommick was womm'ling with hungry. He only had the price of one pint in his pocket so he cude'n buy nothin' to ait in the pub. However, he veeled sure he'd vind zummin putt out on the table.

But 'twad'n true.

His missis had gone to bed and when he went to the larder there wad'n a sign of nothin' aitable. The vire had gone out and no sticks carr'd een, so he took and went to bed likewise.

Nex' mornin' he lied on a hour extry cus he had'n got to go to work, and when he went down over stairs he was fit to ait a man off his hoss. But there wad'n no brekfas', and no likelihoods o' none.

"I'll let 'ee zee who's maister in thees houze," says Dan'l, and he sought about fer his wive. But her'd sent off the chillern to skule and gone to Brattery Manor fer the day, and took the baby along with her.

Dan'l furraged about fer zummin to ait but he cude'n vind so much as a crist o' braid. The inzide aw'n was properly rattlin' fer emptiness. By the middle o' the vorenune he was sick hungerd. He'd alwis bin in the habit o' gwain into the kitchin to the Manor at leb'm 'clock and aitin' a hunch o' braid and chaise. He cude'n bear the thoughts aw't, so he made his way to the gardens and picked up the hoe and started on the turmits, so's he cude knock off fer 'leb'mses as usual.

But he had'n bin to work many minutes when the haid gardener come along.

" Ullaw! What be you doin' yer ? "

" Workin'," says Dan'l.

" No you ban't, you'm trespassin'. Clear off, bevore I putts the policeman after 'ee."

" 'Tis all right, Mr. Barrett, zur. I ban't on strike now."

" Well, I be, then. You jacked up your job and I've got a fresh chap comin', so you skid-daddle, as soon as you like, or a bit sooner."

Dan'l pleaded with 'n, but the haid gardener turned 'n off, 'cus that's what the lady had instructed 'n to do. Dan'l made his way up to the big houze, proper desprit, and the fust thing he zee'd was his missis sot down to a plate of cold bafe and pickle ing'ens. The smell o' they ing'ens made cold watter rin down his teeth.

" Where's squire to ? " he saith.

" He'm to the police coort, jidgin' the rogues what be too idle to work."

'Twad'n in Lisbeth Partridge's heart to spaik to Dan'l like it, fer her was fond aw'n, let be what it may. But Mrs. Brattery had drummed it into her haid that if her did'n do it now her never wude'n.

With the zame in come the lady herzelf.

" What be you doin' around yer, Partridge ? I thought you'd left the squire."

Dan'l cude'n stand no more. The sight o' the bafe and pickle ing'ens had undermined his constitution, as the sayin' is, and he plop right down in a cheer in the face o' the squire's wive.

"If you'll plaise to ax his worship to look over it thees time, mam, and 'low me to come back I'll promish 'ee he'll never have cause to complain again. I bin a fule."

"You have bin a fule, Partridge, and you fergets that other people has got the right to strike as well as you. But I'll zee you has another chance fer the zake of Lisbeth and the chillern."

Lisbeth stood up in her place. "Come and ait this, Dan'l. I dersay you'm in need aw't."

Dan'l got up out of his cheer with his eyes poppin' out of his haid. And then zummin come over 'en, and he stapped short.

"I ban't, I know. I've bin havin' your share years enough. I'll go and finish me job, fust, and then I shall be intitled to it."

And her cude'n turn 'n from it. He went back to his turmit hoein', and did'n straighten his back once fer the rest o' the day. Lisbeth sent up a bit o' dinner fer 'n, by the li'l maid in a bag, and the stoobid feller carr'd it home tay-time in his pocket. But he et a meal then, by jo.

The haid gardener said he never had a rap o'

turmits hoed better, and he did'n have cause to complain of Dan'l arterwards. In fac', the squire have been able to rise Dan'l's wages twice since then, so his lightnin' strike was a success arter all.

IX

WHEN JAN PLAYED FOOTBALL

DON'T talk to me about yer ole vootball. I've had all the vootball I wants, thank you. I took part in it once, and I bet a guinea I'll never do such thing again. How I come to be such a fule as to have aught to do with it, I can't think. However, it larned me a lesson, to laive alone things you don't understand; so I s'pose it done zome gude in a sort of a way. But 'twas a sort of a way I shude'n like very auf'n.

I'd no business bein' there, 't all. If I'd bide home about me work 'twude never have happened. But they made such a fuss about Muddlecombe parish havin' a vootball match, which such a thing had never happened bevore, that I must go and view it like the rest o' the gawks. Why they shude drop 'pon me like they did I can't tell 'ee, 'cus I never done none aw'm no harm that I knows by.

'Twas our chaps agin the Barleycombe chaps, and 'twas only natteral that us shude wish to zee the Muddlecombe lot ween, though what they had to do to bate the other lot I did'n know no more 'n Adam. I did'n know no more about vootball than a cat knows about his awn gran'mother. But I knows now, begad. At laiste, I knows all I wants to know, and in future I'll be satisfied to go down to the Black Oss and play rings. That's more in my line, and not so likely to spoil my buty.

'Twas a vine day fer't, so I pokied away down to Varmer Grant's ten-acre vield to zee this-yer vootball match they was tellin' so much about, never mis-trustin' nothin'. Soon's I got there, the feller they calls the cap'm come rishin' up to me in a joost of a swat.

"Jan," he says, "one of our chaps have bin took bad with a pain in his stommick and he can't play. You mus' come and take the place of 'en."

Of coorse, if I'd had any sainse I wude 'a-bin took bad with a pain in the stommick likewise, but I did'n think aw't in time.

I made all the excuse I cude think of, but they gurt mump'aids wude'n harken to me. They tooked me into Varmer's kitchen and trigged me out in a stoobid ole shurt, like Josep's coat o' many colours, and a li'l ole pair o' short burches which did'n raiche down to me knees. Wad'n hardly dacent, I don't reckon they was, not fer a man my age. I looked like one o' they zebra things, stood up on his hine legs.

"Whatever's the gude?" I says. "You'm only makin' fules o' yerzel's and me too. I dunnaw nothin' about yer ole vootball, and I don't want to vind out, nuther."

But I might as well knack me haid up agin the wall as spaik to they fellers.

"'Tis fer the honour o' the parish, Jan," they said. "Us muzzen let they Barleycombe chaps crow over we. And there won't be very much fer you to do. Us don't want you to do no rinnin' about. Us wants you to be gold-keeper."

"That'll suit me zac'ly," I says. "You bring along the gold, I'll keep it."

Wull, so then the cap'm feller took me over-cross to where they gold paustis was to. They wad'n gold 't all. Only ole timbern paustis, that's all they was; two sticked up about a lan'yard apart, and one across the tap. He was up—aw, what wude he be? Wull, jist up where I cude'n raiche 'n, he was.

"Now, Jan," they said to me, "all you got to do is to bide yer and not let the ball go past 'ee."

"Sounds all right," I said. And nothin' more wad'n said about it.

Then the vootballin' chaps scattered theirzels about all over the plaace. Our lot was decorated up with blue and yaller strips across their chestis, and tother fellers had got rid and black. That's so they cude distinct one from tother. Then there was one li'l feller about half-ways up, he had'n got nothin' seps a wissle. What I mean to say, he had'n got none o' they purty colours. He only weared the zame togs what he had on every day. Only he had this-yer wissle and he keep blowin' chunes on 'en. What he was there 't all vor I dunnaw, cus he wad'n a particle o' gude, and only got in tother volks's way.

When they was all in raddiness, this-yer li'l feller blowed up a bit of a chune, and in one minute they was all rishin' about like a parcel o' rabbuts. I was glad as a burd they putt me in gold-keeper, cus I had'n got nothin' to do seps to watch the tother fellers rinnin' about.

Presen'ly I zee'd one li'l chap rinnin' along by hiszelf. Caw! I never zee'd anybody rin like it in my life. Gwain like one train, he was. One o' they rid and black fellers he was. Stranger to me. I never zee'd the feller bevore in me life that I knows by. But my days, he cude rin. And he'd got the ball along with 'n, too. Aw, 'ees. Ball and all.

Wull, then, sevver'l of our chaps went arter this-yer li'l feller to try and take the ball away from 'en. 'Twas our ball, mind. He had'n got no more right to 'en than what you have, not a bit more. But they cude'n ketch 'en He was too vast fer they. Comin' right towards me he was, too, so I had a splendid view of 'en.

Wull, and I was takin' interest in this-yer li'l chap. I was lookin' to zee how fur he cude rin like it. However, when he thought he'd rinned fur nuff he stapped, and up with his voot, and he gived a kick to thikky ball—— My dear zaul! If he did'n zend 'en jis' like a shot out from a gun. Wull, went right past where I was to. So that'll show 'ee.

Mind you, I thought the feller might jist as well look and zee where he was kickin' of 'n to. 'Twas very careless of 'en, kickin' of 'n so close to me. 'Cus 'twad'n as if he did'n know I was there. 'Twas the luckiest thing in the world I wad'n stood a bit further over. If I had 'a-bin I shude never have escaped 'n.

Wull, then all they rid and black fellers started jumpin' up and down and holleyin' out, "Gold, gold." Proper delighted with theirzels they was. What vor I dunnaw. But our chaps come around me and started spaikin' proper cross to me. Spesh'ly that-there cap'm feller. Properly rude I reckon he was.

"Why had'n 'ee stop 'n, Jan?" he says. "Why had'n he stop 'n?"

"Stop what?" I says.

"Why, the ball, yer silly fule. Why, fer gudeness' sake, had'n 'ee stop 'n ?"

"If he wanted me to stop 'n," I says, "why did'n he kick 'n yer, where I cude raiche 'n, not all out there, zix voot away."

"Aw, you gurt gawk," he says. "He don't want 'ee to stop 'n, but us do. You must dap about a bit and not let the ball go past 'ee."

"Wull, why had'n 'ee told a feller zo? But 'tis no gude you vindin' fau't with me. You want to spaik to that li'l rid and black feller. He kick 'n, I did'n."

With the zame the feller in the middle blowed up another chune on his wissle, and away-to-go, worse 'n ever.

Bim-bye I zee'd the zame li'l chap comin' again. Ball and all.

"All right me li'l feller," I says. "Not this time."

So I went over where I considered the ball was comin' to—well, zame place he come bevore, then, and I got mezelf all in raddiness for 'n and spraid out me arms. But do you know, that li'l chait (that ever I shude say sitch thing), instead of he kickin' the ball to me as he shude 'a-done, he kick 'n zide ways. Wull, there was another rid and black feller stood over there. He wad'n nothin' to do wai't, he wad'n. 'Twas me and the li'l chap, zee.

Wull, and o' cou'se, the other feller he putt his voot to the ball and jis' touched 'n, and in he goes, right droo the gold. There wad'n nothin' to stop 'n.

Then all they rid and black fellers started dancin' up and down again, and holleyin' "Gold, gold."

"Yer," I says, "that wad'n fair," I says. "I wad'n lookin' that way."

"Aw," they said, "you mus' be lookin' every way."

"How many pair of eyes do a feller have on thees job, then?" I says. "What you wants yer is a spider."

Arter that there wad'n a minute's paice. They rid and black chaps was better vootballers than what our fellers was and they keeped on comin' down and tryin' to kick the ball droo my gold. Spesh'ly that li'l feller they called inzide-out. A proper nuisance he was, 'cus he wad'n satisfied when he'd done it once. He must keep on comin' and tryin' to do it again.

"Why don't that li'l feller sit down," I says, "and let zome other body have a go at it?"

"Aw," they says to me, "he played fer the Cristial Palace once."

"Aw, did 'er?" I says. "Well, if he rinned about like he have to-day he deserved to get it, too."

Wull, twad'n very long bevore I zee'd Mr. Inzide-out comin' again, and zame time I zee'd his partner comin' along with 'n.

"I'll be upzides with 'ee this time," I says.

So what I done, I went over to one zide, jis' pretendin' like, till I zee'd the li'l feller was gwain to kick 'n across to his partner. The minute he putt his voot to the zide o' the ball I dapped across tother zide, just in time——

Wull, purty near.

But not quite.

You zee, where 'twas to, 'twas like this-yer. I wad'n hardly so dapper gettin' across as what I ordained fer to be, and that feller give the ball a kick like a mule.

I wad'n quick nuff to stop 'n with me hands.

I stop 'n with me faace.

BANG.

Aw, my dear zaul! I thought it never wude be a faace again. I did'n know what had happened. I cude'n zee; ner I cude'n yer; ner I cude'n spaik. I putt up me hand to the back o' me haid to zee if me nawse had come out behind.

And when I beginned to braithe again and got one eye open the cap'm feller come up to me and said:

"Bravo, Jan; bravo. You stopped that one butiful."

" Aw," I says. " What did I stop ? "

" Why, you stopped the ball."

" Is that all? I thought I'd stopped a sharrybang."

" Look out, Jan. They'm comin' again."

" Aw, be um ? " I says. " Wull, you come and putt your faace yer. I'm takin' mine home."

X

THE COUNCIL ELECTION

THAT was the master caper when they had the Council 'Lection to Barleycombe. I've zee'd a vew upstores in my time, but I'm jiggered if that did'n top the lot. From what I can understand, Town Council 'Lection ought to come around every Fust o' November, but as a rule the Barleycombe volk don't pay no more attention to it than they do to the weend blowin'. The time comes and goes jis' the zame as Gude-a-Vridy or pancake day and no notice took of it, fer the simple raison that nobody troubles to disturb the mimbers on the council. There they be, and there they have-a-bin fer dunkey's years, and there they'm likely to stap, fer all anybody cares. Nobody else id'n ambitious to take the place of 'em.

I dunnaw that they'm very much gude, but they ban't very much harm, and they comes in handy to find fau't with when aught goes wrong with the drains, or if there's too much rain vor the crops, or a long dryth and the watter rins short, or when zome other body's haidges be growed out over the rawd, or you receives a order to trim back yer own. 'Tis gude to have zomebody to putt the blame on to, and that's where councils comes in useful I reckon. But 'tis a seldom thing anybody covets bein' a mimber, so the zame lot goes on from one year to the next.

Until this-yer rumpus took place into the Golden Lion. That's where it started to, into the Golden Lion. That's where most things starts to which id'n very much credic to nobody.

I can't tell 'ee zac'ly who sot the ball rollin', 'cus one says one thing and one says another, and you dunnaw which to believe. But I *do* know that Benjamin Tolley and Zam Partridge both happened to be in there one aiv'min and had a tremenjis argiment. 'Tis a very seldom thing you'll vind Benjamin in any such place, I will say that much vor 'en, but whether 'tis becus he don't take very much to drink, or whether 'tis becus he's too near to pay vor't I won't say. As fer Zammy, if he id'n in the Golden Lion you can bet a guinea he's eetherways into the Vox an' Geeze or else into the Half Mune.

Be that as it may, on this pa'ticler occasion Zammy Partridge was callin' the council all the rogues and thaves on the face of the earth.

I dunnaw what 'twas about, zac'ly, but from what I can make out the council had ordered Zammy to repair a bit o' rawd, and they told 'n that if he did'n do it they wude, and charge he the cost aw't. Zammy was proper furious, and he was raycallin' the council zummat hawful when Benjamin looked in and yer'd what he was sayin'. Of coorse, Benjamin have bin a mimber o' the council ever since he was a youngish man, and now he've got a long white beard down to his watch chain. He've been a shoemaker and a local praicher in his time, so you mid be sure he id'n lost fer words, and he very zoon give Zammy back as gude as he brought. So there was a middlin' vine racket between the two aw'm.

And arter they'd bin gwain hammer and tongs fer ever so long, both shoutin' the top o' their voice and neether-one harkening to what the tother was sayin', Benjamin says:

"Look at yer, Zam Partridge, you've got so much to say about how the council shude carry on, why don't you stand vor mimber and bring forth zome o' thase-yer wonderful projec's instaid o' critickisin' other people. 'Tis all very well fer you to zit yer in public-houze telling about the council ought to do this and council did'n ought to do that, but you takes gude care you daun' take no part yerzelf, daun' 'ee?"

"Me, be on the council!" says Zammy. "Why, gude lor, I've got dree cats and a black rabbut up to my place and I cude make a better council out o' they than all you lot putt together."

"In that case," says Benjamin, "you can't have so much sainse as the rabbut, fer certin, else you'd putt up fer council yerzelf."

"Sainse! Tid'n sainse you chaps have got up there to the council, 'tis chick. That's all that got 'ee there, is chick; to think you'm fit to make rules and regillations over and above yer feller men. Darn chick, that's all you've got. Sainse is what you *wants*, mister."

"Then why don't you bring along zome, zeeing you've got so much aw't. Any fule can bide yer and find fau't with what other volks be doing. But if you'm so much more clever than all the rest you shude putt up fer council and let the town have the benevit aw't. You'm like the squaik in the weel-barra; you makes all the noise and you don't assist in the work. You sticks in this-yer parler and tells about the wonderful idayas you've got in yer haid, but you'm feared to come up to the council chamber and putt 'em out like a man."

"Feared, be I? My gudeness gracious! Zummat to be feared of, you lot be, I'm pippered. I shude make zome o' the rest of 'ee feared purty quick if I was up there amongs' 'ee very long."

"Yas. I've yer'd ducks quack bevore. You takes gude care you don't try it on, though."

"And do you know why, Benjamin Tolley? Do you know why I never stood fer council?"

"Yas. Certinly I do. Becus you knows very well nobody wude'n vote fer 'ee."

Caw! My dear zaul! There was proper pandymonian then. Everybody in the rume joined it, and zome was fer Benjamin and zome was fer Zammy. But they was only pretendin', all the lot of 'em, and edgin' they two on, jus' fer wickedness.

"I'm bothered if I'd have a thing like that said about me, Zammy," says Georgie Gurnslade. "I shude 'a-thought there'd be all-so-many vote fer you as fer Mr. Tolley."

"A sight more, my son," says Zammy. "I'll make a bet if 'twas a vight between me and he, he wude'n have a smell to it."

Then there was another upstore, everybody shoutin' to-once.

"Stap a minute!" Bill Maddick 'olleyed out. "Hold thee baal, all of 'ee, and harken to what I've got to say. I've jus' thought o' zummin. Id'n it your turn to come off the council this time, Mr. Tolley?"

"What do 'ee mean, Mr. Maddick?"

"Why, unless I'm very much mistook, your dree years is up, now this November. You've got to putt up to be 'lected again, ab'm 'ee?"

"Us never don't," says Benjamin, lookin' mortle uncomferable. "Tid'n the custom with the Barleycombe Council, without anybody wants to retire."

"I know 'tid'n the custom," says Wi'yum. "But that's only becus nobody else don't putt up fer council, which is the very thing you'm grousin' about. You say that they what ban't satisfied with the present members shude try it theirzels. I agrees with you. I'm same opinion, zac'ly. Well, now, your time shude be up now shortly, and I reckon, after all the things he've had to say about you, Zammy Partridge shude stand agin 'ee, and let the people say which they thinks is the better man. That's my regards in the matter; I dunnaw what the rest thinks about it."

No need vor me to tell 'ee what the rest thought about it. They zee'd a chance fer zome purty vine rigs and they wad'n gwain to let it go if they cude help aw't. Zammy tried to back out, but they wude'n let 'n to. Bill Maddick's a rare hand fer a job o' that sort. 'Twas just his han'writin'.

"Bide quiet, all of 'ee," he says. "I've knowed Zam Partridge all the days of his life and he id'n the sort o' chap that's gwain to run word ; you need'n be 'feared o' that. When Mr. Partridge have said a thing his word's as gude as his bound. And when he says he'll putt up fer Council there id'n a man in Barleycombe or any place else is gwain to frighten 'en from it. He id'n afraid o' Mr. Tolley ner no other man. They both belongs to Lowertown, so 'twill be a straight vight between 'em, and may the best man ween."

Of coorse, Zammy had'n said no such thing, railly, but he did'n like to dray back, feared they'd make a laafin' sport of 'n. And so they had 'n nonimated, or whatever they calls it, and then there was middlin' vine works to Barleycombe fer a wik or two. Benjamin Tolley and Zammy Partridge was took more notice of vor the nex' vortnit than they was all the rest o' their life, and by the time the 'lection was over neether-one aw'm did'n have nuff chara'ter left to wrap up his lunch in.

Bills was sticked up on all the walls and double doors, " Vote fer Tolley " or " Vote fer Partridge," and the li'l boys drayed the images of the candidates on 'em with blacklead pencils and wrote down remarks about 'em which wad'n intended to be kind. 'Twas the only topic the volks told about. Even when they come out from prayer of a Zindy they did'n discuss the sarment. 'Twas all whether Benjamin Tolley wude go back on the council again or whether Zam Partridge wude oust 'n out from it. 'Twas better 'n a penny-raidin' to go into eether o' the publics and yer the argifyin' between the Tolleys and the Partridges.

And people wad'n very pa'ticler what they said about the two candidates, neether. They what was fer Zammy cude'n vind nothin' bad nuff to zay about Benjamin. There was Georgie Gurnslade fer one.

"How anybody with a hattom o' sainse cude vote fer Benjamin Tolley," he says, "I can't think. He ab'm got the brains of a tom-tit. What have he done fer the gude of the town since he've bin on the council? You might jis-so-well putt in thikky quart pot. Better in fac', 'cus there is zummin inside the quart pot, or there was till Jim Pike putt his face to 'en. But what is there in Ben Tolley? Nort but a parcel of sankeymonious ole chapel-trade. He'm the miserablest ole toad on the face of the earth hiszelf, and if he had his way he'd make every other body miserable likewise. They say his own gran'mother had to be putt away to 'sylum and 'tis my opionion he ought to be there hiszelf. I s'pause he reckons he'll be the Mayor o' Barleycombe bim-bye if he bides on the council long nuff, and then he'll be Jistice o' the

Paice, begad, and have the jidgment of you an' me. Caw, dally, he'll putt everybody to prisin what don't go about with a face as long as dree fiddles."

Then zome other body wude crack off about Zammy.

"Purty vine objic' to be on the council he is. Nort but a proper rinagate. Twice his vather was putt to prisin fer pauchin', and the zame wude have happened to he only he ve had the gude luck not to be ketched. What about he fer a jidge of his feller men?"

And so it went on; zome makin' out that Zammy or Ben was anjels and tothers makin' 'em to be the scum o' the earth.

But the meetin' they held topped the lot. Of coorse, neether Zammy ner Benjamin did'n want no meetin', and they wude'n have had none if they'd had their own way. But they did'n have their own way. Bill Maddick zee'd to that. He ingaged Lowertown Parish Hall and had notices sticked about all over the place that the two candidates wude address the 'lecters on Zaturdy night. Soon's Benjamin heard about it he went rinnin' along to Mr. Maddick.

"I ban't gwain to address no 'lecters. I ban't gwain to address no 'lecters. I shan't do nothin' o' the sort. Such thing have never bin done bevore in Barleycombe and I ban't gwain to do it."

"All right, Mr. Tolley. If you mind to make Zam Partridge a presint of your sate on the council all well and gude. Zammy will go in flyin'. Of coorse he will, 'cus all the volks will say you had'n got the courage to putt out your views so they can't be worth havin'."

"But Partridge id'n gwain to make a spaich?"

"Aw, id'n ee, begad? Zammy's gwain to make a butiful spaich. I'll make a bet 'twill be a spaich that wude get'n in Parlyment, never mind about Barleycombe council."

"Well, I s'pause if he do I must. But 'tis a parcel of tomfulishness, all the lot aw't."

And Benjamin wad'n hardly gone out o' sight bevore in comes Zammy.

"What's the meanin' o' this ole witpot? I ban't gwain to make no spaich."

"Then you can zay 'Gude-by' to any hopes o' gettin' on the council, Zammy. Mr. Tolley is larnin' his spaich now, and I'll make a bet he'll make up a butiful peeration."

"Aw, well, if he do, I s'pause I must."

And zo they had the meetin', and I'm jiggered if twad'n a proper pantomine. The place was so full you cude hardly braithe, 'cus there wad'n nothin' to pay to go een. And all the hobbidy-hoys o' the place was stood back behind or sot up in the winders.

Colonel Brown was the cheerman, and the paasen and sevver'l more o' the better-most volk was sot on the platvorm. The cheerman made the two candidates toss up who shude go fust, and he said the lot had valled on Mr. Tolley. And 'twas a lot, I'm bothered if 'twad'n.

So Benjamin got up on his hine legs, lookin' turrable uncomferable. There was a middlin' gude racket, drec'ly. Zome volks clapped their hands, and the chaps back behind zinged out "Maa," 'cus they reckons that Ben's wiskers makes 'n look like a billy-goat. And o' cou'se, every time they done that there was a roar o' laafin'.

I can't tell 'ee much what Ben did say, cus there was such noise gwain on I cude'n ketch half aw't. And 'twad'n a gurt lot when 'twas all putt together. He was swattin' down strames although 'twas a coldish night.

"I've bin thirty years on the council," he says, "and what have I done?"

"Nort," says zomebody drec'ly and the place properly shook with the laafture.

"I ab'm done nothin' that I be 'shamed of," says Benjamin.

"You ab'm had a shave," goes zomebody else, and then they all laafed again. So then Colonel Brown stood up to ax fer gude order. But one o' the chaps holleyed out:

"Stan' at ease!"

'Twas the colonel's voice, zac'ly, and everybody roared. So the cheerman got very rid in the faace and sot down again. Then Benjamin had another go to it, but he cude'n get vore very well 'cus he'd fergot what he intended to say, and he yammered and kickied, and then zomebody said, "Spit it out, uncle," and there they was as bad as ever.

Then Benjamin lost his timper and said 'twas a pity zome aw'm did'n know the way to behave theirzels. That only made the hobbidy-hoys wiss than bevore, and every wips-wile one aw'm wude shout across the rume:

"Why don't you behave yourzelf, Tom Aish? I'll tell your mother o' you."

That wude be a vine joke and they'd all bust out laafin'. Spesh'ly the maidens. They was all-so-bad as the chaps. So then Benjamin got flummoxed and stood there properly mum. Everybody got quiet to yer what he was gwain say next, but he cude'n get a word out. The place was silent as a church, but still poor Ben cude'n make a sound, and then all-to-once Percy Shute shouted up, " Zing it, maister."

That putt the finisher on it. The volks laafed till they nearly cried, and then Ben sot down. The chaps to the back o' the rume all zinged, " Fer he's a jolly gude feller," but they only done it out o' wickedness.

So then the cheerman called upon Zammy to spaik. But Zammy was frightened out of his life, zeein' what Benjamin had to go droo, and he got on wiss than tother chap. I never yer'd two words of what he said, 'cus the chaps was warmed up by thees time and they led poor Zammy a proper dance.

And when he sot down the cheerman stood up and said us had yer'd the two candidates and 'twas fer the 'lecters to decide which one they wude vote fer. And he was jis' 'pon the point o' sayin' the meetin' was all over, when the paasen wispered in his yer'ole. So the cheerman announced that the vicar wude say a vew words.

The paasen said, " Ladies an' gen'lmen. I've got a li'l surprise fer 'ee. Us considered us had to pick between the two gen'lmen which have spoke yer to-night, but I understand another candidate is to be denominated and wude like to say a few words if you wish it."

Everybody was flabbergasted, but us all give a gude clap, 'cus us was havin' a very gude time and wude be glad to yer zome more aw't. So the paasen stood one zide and up staps Miss Margaret Ammitt to Winscot.

Us cude scarcely believe our eyes. Of cou'se, us knowed there *was* such things as women puttin' up fer council, but us had never zee'd one bevore. But there her was, stood there smilin' and cule as a cowcumber. And bevore any o' the chaps cude think of aught to say her started spaichifyin'.

And 'twas some spaich, my word. Her never had so much as a scrip o' paper ner nort, but her went right a-haid wai't and never stapped fer a word. One or two o' the chaps tried to putt in their funny remarks, but her picked 'em up so quick and made 'em look that fulish, everybody laafed at they instead o' laafin' at the spaiker, and they got frightened to open their mouthe. Her rattled it off fer vive an' twenty minutes by the clock, and Benjamin Tolley sot there with his mouthe open so wide his wiskers was all two-double on his chest, and Zammy's eyes was like tay-sassers.

So they had the 'lection, and when Mr. Richards gived out the viggers from the winder to the Gill'all, 'twas—Margaret Ammitt, 481; Benjamin Tolley, 57; Zamuel Partridge, 22.

Benjamin said he lost becus everybody was so sure he'd get in they thought they'd give Miss Ammitt jis' one vote to help her along. Zammy said 'twas all done through bigamy and corruption.

XI

SPECIAL LICENCE

LIAS BUZZACOTT was a turrable chap for playin' up thase-yer pra'tical jokes. Nothin' plaised he better than makin' other volks look more fulish than what they railly was. Where he got all his stoobid idayas to I can't think. I suppose it must be like Mrs. Endycott said: not havin' very much sainse in his haid there was all the more room fer the nonsainse.

The amazin' part aw't was, Lias cude make people believe all manner of redic'lus things without acsh'ly sayin' aught that wad'n true. That was the annoyin' thing about it. After anybody had bin made a fule of they'd go up to Lias next time they zee'd 'n, and say to 'en, "What do you mean by tellin' me such lies?"

"What lies?" says Lias. "I never told 'ee no lies."

And when they comes to think it back over they'm bound to admit that Lias is right. He never said what they thought he said.

"Folks muzzen blame me," says Lias, "if they putts two and two together and makes vive aw't. That's their awn look out. And if they had'n got wrong minds they wude'n think wrong things."

Of coorse, he's only laafin' up his sleeve at 'ee. But there 'tis. You can't prove nothin' up agin 'en. That's where his artfulness comes een.

Look at that caper of Mark Bawden's weddin'; or supposed to be Mark Bawden's weddin'. You might say there was half the parish made to look fulish, but 'twas impossible to putt the blame on Lias. Other people got accused fer that; and when come all-to-all you cude'n say but what they dezerved it. Spesh'ly Sophy Grinnaway. But I'll tell 'ee all the rigmarole and then you can zee fer yerzelf.

But fust of all you mus' know zummin about Mark Bawden and likewise about Sophy Grinnaway, else you won't understand the joke proper.

Mark was a old boye, or what zome people terms a bacheler. 'Twad'n only that he never got married, but he objected to women altogether. He wude'n have none about his plaace, ner he wude'n spake to one if he cude help aw't. He lived all by hiszelf in a li'l houze up-top the heel, and although 'twas knawed he'd got a-plenty o' money, 'twas a seldom thing he went out, and he never took part in nothin' that was gwain on in the village. Proper ole mizer he was, and zome volks went so fur as to say he was a witch.

Wull, and o' cou'se, Mrs. Grinnaway was exac'ly the oppozyte. Her had her nawse in everybody's business. Her alwis went by the name o' the "Muddlecombe Daily News," cus her knawed every bit o' gossip that was gwain about. And if her did'n knaw it her wude'n rest till her did. If any wumman in the plaace wanted to yer the latest about anybody her'd fly to Sophy, and if Sophy did'n know nothin' her'd very zoon hatch zummin up.

However! One day the paasen stapped Lias in the rawd. Day avore Lady Day 'twas. I knaw that, 'cus Varmer George Westaway was movin' into Town Livin' and Lias was helpin' aw'n to shift his things.

"Shall you be doin' anythin' to-morra wik, Lias?" says the paasen.

"Nothin' pa'ticler that I knaws by, zur."

"Well, I'll tell 'ee what I wants. The dean is comin' out to view the ole brass in the church and one or two things, and I shude like fer you to drive auver to the station in the waggonet and meet 'n by the nine 'clock train and take 'n back in time to ketch the twelve-thirty, cus

George Sage is bad in bed and I don't think he'll be well nuff to go."

So that's how Lias come to knaw the dean was comin', but he never said a word about it till the day bevore, and then he managed to ketch ole Sophy on the quiet. He made meanings through her winder that he wanted to spake to her, and creeped in the door on the sly, lookin' very mysterious.

"Mrs. Grinnaway," he says, "have you yer'd any saycret business about ole Mark Bawden gettin' married."

Wull, now, Sophy Grinnaway is the last body in the world wude confess her had'n yer'd anything. Her cude'n say, "'Tis news to me," any more than her cude fly. So her said:

"Aw! So it have reached you have it, Lias Buzzacott? How did *you* come to know anything about it?"

Her's a deep ole toad, Sophy is, or her thinks her is, and her alwis reckons to be able to vind out all that anybody knows without lettin' on that her's ignerant aw't herzelf.

"Never mind how I knaws it," says Lias. "I ab'm vound a zingle body what has yer'd about it seps you. But to my mind there's zummin very jubious about it. Why shude the ole feller want to go to the expainse of a speshul licence, instaid o' being called to church for dree Zindys in a proper manner? "

"Very true, Lias," says the ole dumman, properly shakin' with excitement. "That's the very thing I said to mezelf. Why shude he vor? "

"And another thing, Mrs. Grinnaway. Who fer gudeness' saake can he be gwain to marry that the bishop hiszelf shude come all out yer to prevorm the sarrymony? Bishops daun' go to li'l plaaces like this to marry ordnery volk."

"I knaw they don't, Lias. I've racked me brain and I've tried to think who it can be, and fer the life o' me I can't putt a name to her."

"And furthermore, missis," he saith, "why shude they make up their mind all of a sudden like this to be wed of a Saturdy mornin' at tain o'clock? "

"There's zummin very funny about it," her says. "But, o' cou'se, he've alwis bin a very funny sort o' man."

"Anyway," says Lias, "don't say a word about it to a zaul, Mrs. Grinnaway, cus Mark ab'm uttered a zound. 'Tis very plain to zee he don't intend Dick, Tom and 'Arry to know about it. But I think 'twill be worth-a-while to be to the church doors to-morrow mornin' and zee who have managed to ketch the ole feller and his money-bags."

When Lias went away from the door he cude jis' picsher Sophy rishin' to putt on her bonnet and flippin' across the road to Mrs. Zalter's fer a start, and from there to Mrs. Annaford's, and then on to Mrs. Webber's and Mrs. Cann's; into the Paust Orfice; Mrs. Carpenter to the Black Oss; Sarah Tozer to the shop, Jane Ammitt, Poll Bradferd, and so on. Her wude'n be able to stap and yap as long as her'd like to with each one, becus, havin' told 'em all to keep it a saycret she knowed they'd be off to tell zome other body soon's ever her was out the door. And nothin' was more hawful to Sophy than to carr' a tale to anybody and then vind they knowed it a'ready.

And zo Mrs. Grinnaway carr'd around the wonderful news, how that ole Mark Bawden was gwain to be married to-morrow mornin' at tain o'clock by speshul licence and how that the bishop hiszelf was comin' to conduc' the sarvice. The only thing her wude'n tell 'em was the name o' the bride.

"I'd like to tell 'ee, my dear," her said, "but I promished faithful that I wude'n so much as breathe her name. But I can promish 'ee one thing, you'll be very zurprised when you zee who 'tis, and 'twill show 'ee what riches can do even when a man's old and hugly and bad-timpered."

Sophy considered 'twas safe to venter that much.

And by 'ar-pas' nine the nex' mornin' there was bes' part of a score o' volks to the church door. Long bevore tain o'clock half the parish was there, and tother half was on the way, zome with bags o' rice, some with 'ole butes, and hoss-shoes, and some with this-yer confetty trade.

About a quatter bevore tain the paasen and the dean come strollin' up the road from the paasonidge. The dean had got on his black leggin's and his box 'at, so the women-volk said drec'ly :

" Aw, 'tis right, lookee. 'Tis the bishop, sure 'nuff. So it must be true arter all."

" What do you mean, ' true arter all ? ' " says Sophy. " Of cou'se 'tis true. Did you think I was tellin' 'ee lies ? "

Paasen was properly tooked aback to zee so many volks stood around the church doors, and the dean was a bit surprised, speshly when all the women made a bob, thinkin' 'twas the bishop hiszelf. Still, he must 'a-bin plaised to think that the parishioners took so much interest in church matters.

However, they went into the church, and the volks waited anxious fer the bride and bridegrom and discussed the bishop as they thought. Most aw'm was disappointed.

"I did'n think bishops was like that, did you?" says Jane Ammitt. "I alwis thought a bishop was big and vat and had long wiskers."

"Not all of 'em," says Mrs. Martin, who've lived up to Lunnon and knows everything. "It all depends. If they'm low church they wears wiskers but if they'm high church they shaves all their hair off, even on the top o' their 'aids."

The other women didn't believe her a bit, but they cude'n contrydict her. You can't very well contrydict a wumman what have lived up to Lunnon.

When the Church clock strik tain what a consternation there was to be sure.

"Purty vine start fer the bridegroom to be late on his weddin' day," the women-volk said; and the men said, "What about the bride, then? Her's late as well."

There was sever'l men present by thees time, and more comin' along.

"Aw, wull," says the women, "'tis excusable fer the bride. Her's expected to be a bit late jis' to show that her id'n in no gurt hurry to get married."

"Different to my ole wumman, then," says Jim Soper. "Her come around to my place and called fer me on the way to make sure I did'n run word."

"I'll make a bet her've wished ever so many

times since that you had, Jim," says Ernie Cann.

" I dersay her have, Ernie," says Jim. " And if her ab'm, I have."

There was a lot more o' that sort of ole crams, but presen'ly the clock strick quatter past and then they had zummin else to tell about. No weddin' couple had'n arrived and everybody was busy makin' up a raison for't. Poll Bradferd was of opinion that we shude yer of some draidful traggedy bevore long.

Sophy Grinnaway said, " What a turrable scat in the face fer the poor bishop. 'Tis a disgrace it shude have happened in Muddlecombe parish."

Then zomebody else said :

" They'm comin' out again, lookee. I spause the bishop refuses to wait any longer."

And so they was. Paasen and the dean come droo the church door and when they see'd the crowd gathered there they was properly frightened. Sophy walked straight up and spoke to the paasen.

" Beg yer pardon, zur, is the weddin' pos'-ponded ? "

" Weddin', Mrs. Grinnaway," he says. " What weddin' ? "

" Aw, us knows all about it, zur," says Sophy, cus her thought paasen was tryin' to keep it dark like the rest. "I've knowed about it fer a long time. Mr. Mark Bawden, zur. Tain o'clock he was supposed to be yer."

But mind you Sophy's voice beginned to get a bit wobbly-like towards the finish, cus anybody cude zee by the paasen's faace that he was properly lost.

" 'Tis the fust I've yer'd about it, Sophy," he says.

" But did'n his lordship, the bishop, come out yer zame purpose to prevorm the sarrymony ? "

Sophy's voice was like anybody jis' dead, axing fer a drink o' watter.

" This id'n the bishop," he says. " This is the dean."

My days, if you cude only have zeen Sophy's face then, you'd 'a-said zomebody ought to fetch the doctor. And a gude many more was almost as bad, what had done a bit o' runnin' around news-mongerin' on their own account.

Then the dean putt in a word.

" Do you think the date have got aught to do wai't? 'Tis the fust of April, unless I'm mistaken."

My hyvers! April Fule Day!

What upstore there was to be sure, and everybody tryin' to make out they had'n come fer no pa'ticler purpose, but only stapped becus' they zee'd the other volks there. 'Twas amusin' to zee the poor crayters what had got rice and so forth tryin' to hide away their parcels. Poor Mrs. Tolley with one of her husband's ole butes had a turrable job to get 'n out o' zight, cus Dan Tolley have got the biggest veet in the parish.

XII

TALES FROM THE CARRIER'S CART

I. A PARCEL OF TRUMPERY

THERE id'n very many o' the ole fashin carriers' carts left. They'm a thing o' the past. There was a time when a pair of hosses was gude 'nuff to take the volks to market once a wik, and 'most every village had its carrier's cart. And thought a lot of they was, too, cus they was the only means of gettin' into the world, as you might zay. But they ban't vast 'nuff in these days. 'Tis all moters now. Even the country volks is too up-to-date to ride behind hosses. They've got to flip about quick to keep up with the times. And I won't zay but what 'twas a bit tayjis now and then, pokin' along in the ole " Muddlecombe Express " as us used to term it, about as vast as a body cude walk. 'Speshly of a dark, cold winter's mornin', when you cude hardly tell where yer veet ended and the floor beginned.

And yet, zometimes, when I thinks back auver,

I fancies us use to be more sociable-like in they days. Us was packed in tight together, cus there wad'n very much rume to spare 'genst you'd got in all the baskets and parcels and rabbuts and one thing and tother. And us was there fer longer time, so there was more yappin' than what there is now-a-days. I won't say there was alwis a turrable amount o' sainse in the conversation. Zometimes 'twas all a parcel of ole crams. But even fulishness comes in handy zometimes if it makes 'ee laaf, and zome o' the volks what lived in out-the-way places wude have more laafin' in the ole carrier's cart in one day than they wude all the rest o' the wik gwain about their lonely jobs.

'Speshly when you'd got people like Lias Buzzacott and Tom Zalter, and Mrs. Endycott and Mrs. Snell. Wance let 'em start on zome stoopid ole topic and there was no end to the wit-pot they'd tell up.

'Twas so gude as the play when Lias and Mrs. Endycott started on their ole crams. He was a turrifyin' toad if ever there was one. He was everlastin' tryin' to make out that missis intended to have he for her next. Her've bin a widda-wumman fer dunkey's years, and Lias alwis declared her'd got her eye 'pon he for her number two. Of coorse, he only done it to turrify the ole zaul, cus everybody knaws her wude'n be bothered with 'n about the place. And Lias wude'n marry nobody fer certin, cus he'd be feared if he was to he'd have to go to work rigler, whether he wanted to or no. And that wude'n suit Lias in they days. He was a rare chap to work when he veeled like it, but he did'n alwis veel like it.

I minds very well the conversation on one journey, which will show 'ee the sort o' rummage that was told up when us was in the mood fer 't. 'Twas a winter's mornin' I remember, and middlin' yark, and Mrs. Endycott keeped on grum'lin' cus us did'n get along vaster.

"What be grousin' about so much, missis?" says Tom Zalter. "I wonder you daun' get out and walk."

"I wude if I was in a hurry," her says.

"Fust time I knowed you when you wad'n in a hurry," says Tom.

Lias said, "Mrs. Endycott likes gwain slow when her's ridin' cus her gets more fer her money that way."

"But it means puttin' up with you for longer time," her says, "so that's worse again."

"'Tis no use you pretendin' that, missis. You knows very well you'd miss me like anything if I wad'n yer."

"That's right. Same's I shude miss the teeth's-ache arter it got better. A very gude miss."

" You'd soon be wishin' you cude zee me back, Mrs. Endycott."

" I wude'n mind seein' yer back. 'Tis yer faace I objec's to."

" Never mind, missis. I be gwain to take you to the picshers nex' week, when you pays me that sixpence you owes me fer carr'ing they two gurt baskets o' poultry into the station. 'Twill be dark as a bag in there so you won't be able to zee my faace, and us can sit and hold hands all the time instaid."

" My dear zaul, I shude be sorry to have you hold my hand. If you was to hold yer tongue 'twude be a blessin'. But 'tis too late fer that, I'm 'fraid."

" Yas, missis, 'tis too late. I've promised I'd have 'ee and I ban't gwain to run word now."

" What's think o' the gurt gawk, Mr. Annaferd ? " her says. " Did 'ee ever come across sitch a stoopid in all yer life ? "

" Aw, I dunnaw, missis," says Tom Zalter. " You might have zomebody worse than Lias."

" I dersay I might," her says, " but I hope to gudeness I shan't. Nor not half so bad. 'Twude be a poor come-along-aw't, sure 'nuff."

" That's all very well," says Tom. " You tells like that in front o' we, but how do us know what things you say to the feller when you'm alone ? "

" Very true, Tom," says Lias. " You wude'n

believe the nice things her says to me when there's nobody about."

"No," he says. "I shude be sorry to believe anything you told me fer certin."

Ole Tom's a begger like that. You never knaws whe'er he'm gwain to back 'ee up or no. As long as he can have his li'l joke he daun' care whe'er 'tis you or tother feller. You might think he'm on your zide and gwain to uphold 'ee to the huttermost and all of a sudden he'll turn right round and set everybody laafin' at 'ee.

"I knows what's the matter with you, Tom Zalter," says Lias. "You'm jellis, that's what you be. Jellis, 'cus you thought Mrs. Endycott was gwain to wait fer you, and you don't like it now her's mazed about me."

"Hold thee baal, for gudeness' sake," says Mrs. Endycott. "Anybody wude need to be mazed fer certin to want to be plagued with a half-bake like you. You might come in handy fer a mommet, praps, to frighten the burds away. That's about the most thing you'm fit for."

"You wude'n think that missis was haid over heels in love with me, to yer her talk, wude 'ee?" says Lias. "But her is, you know. Her only says things like that jis' to putt 'ee off the track, like. But I can tell by the look in her eyes, when her just glimpses me zometimes. Like if I goes to church, her'll keen across to me every wips-wile when the rest o' the volks has got their eyes shut, and the look her gives me makes me go preckles all over. 'Tis that lovin' you can't think."

"And what do you look like, Lias?" axed Ned.

"Like a gurt fule, same's he do any other time," says Mrs. Endycott.

"No, I'll tell 'ee what I looks like," says Lias. "I looks at her as gude as to say, 'That'll be the time, my dear, when me and you comes to church and sits together in the same sate, and all the volks wispers to one-tother, 'What a hansum couple they makes, daun' 'um?' Missis knows what I means when I gives her that sort o' look, and her blushes right down to the knuckle end of her nose. And mind you, Mrs. Endycott looks a proper picsher when her blushes. You wude'n believe the differnce. Just give a li'l bit of a blush now, Mrs. Endycott, and let em' zee how it suits 'ee."

Mrs. Snell said, "Give the gurt gawk a gude lerrickin' with yer umberella, Mrs. Endycott. I shude, I know."

But missis did'n wan not tellin'. There wad'n rume inzide the cart to give 'n a proper scat but her let'n have such a pug in the zide with the point of her umberella, I'll make a bet he had the mark there fer a vortnit. And a fat lot o' gude it done 'en.

"There you be, Tom Zalter," he says. "What did I tell 'ee! She wude'n behave like that to me if she wad'n very fond of me. 'Tis the way missis shows her love. 'Tis more than her've ever done fer you."

"Ees, and more than her'd ever better-way try to," says Tom. "If that's her manner of showin' her love, you'm very welcome, thank you."

"Aw, bless yer 'art, her'll make that all up bim-bye. And that's the best part aw't; id'n it, Mrs. Endycott, the makin' up part?"

"I'll give 'ee the feller scat to the last one if you don't take care," her said. "And the nex' one will be a lot harder, mind, and in a softer spot, cus I shall give 'ee a poke in the head."

"Of cou'se, her don't like to make it up before all you lot," says Lias. "But you ought to zee her when you ban't lookin'."

"How cude us see her if us ban't lookin', mump'aid?" says Mrs. Snell.

"Let's know when 'tis comin' off, Lias," says Ned; "so's us can zend 'ee a weddin' present."

"I shall let 'ee know all right, maister. Us be gwain to send around they li'l picshers, like the gen'lvolks do, with a couple of hearts and a skivver through 'em. One heart will be mine and other Mrs. Endycott's."

Mrs. Snell said, " What'll yours be, a sheep's heart, Lias ? "

" Yas, missis. And he'll be stuffed with traicle to show he'm a switheart."

" Better-way, putt on a sheep's haid as well," said Mrs. Endycott, " with the brains took out, and then they'll know tis' you fer certin."

Tom Zalter said, " I s'pause you'll have black around the vorridge o' they cards, Lias ? "

" To be sure, maister. And ' No flowers by requess '."

" And 'R.I.P.'," says Ned Annaferd.

" What do that stand vor ? "

" Rest in Paice."

" Aw, well, us'll leave that off. There won't be no rest fer me, and darn little paice, that's for certin. 'Speshly when 'tis 'ogs-puddens fer dinner."

" What have that got to do with it ? "

" Well, you zee, missis is very partial to 'ogs-puddens, so her'd give me a very li'l paice and her'd have all the rest."

" Yer us be, into Exeter," says Mrs. Endycott. " Lias Buzzacott, you can carr' that heaviest basket o' mine up to the market for yer chick, and praps, bim-bye, I might invite 'ee to drink yer awn health. 'Tis to be hopes 'twill be the nearest you ever gets to a wedding toast—for the sake of yer wife."

Dear, dear! What a parcel of ole trumpery. But I wude'n say but what us got through the day all the better fer startin' with a gude laaf.

2. TOM ZALTER'S DAY'S PLEASURE

"What's matter with you 's-mornin', Tom Zalter? I fancy you'm lookin' turrable wishy-washy."

"I shude'n be at all surprised, Mrs. Snell. I'm *feelin'* wishy-washy."

"You wants a 'olladay, that's what you wants."

"No, I don't want nothin' o' the sort, missis. That's the very thing I *don't* want, becus I've had one."

"You've had a 'olladay? When was that then?"

"I had one yesterday, missis; and that's what's the matter."

"Aw, get out with 'ee! What's one day's 'olladay? You wants a month."

"I shude never last out the time, Mrs. Snell. A month's 'olladay is all very well fer they what can afford to have a gude rest afterwards to get over it. Us have got a sample of 'em up to our place now."

"Have your wife got people in, then?"

"Yas, Mrs. Snell. Us have got vive aw'm there, from up-the-country zomewhere. They goes by differ'nt discriptions, accordin' to who's tellin' about 'em. They terms theirzels visiters; my missis refers to 'em as boarders; I calls 'em lodgers; and Poll Bradferd what comes twice a week to help clean up the mess behind 'em calls 'em everything but what they was christened. And of coorse, with so much ole wet weather, day arter day, and so many of 'em plattin' in and out, they makes a tidy muck about the plaace.

"However, they'm supposed to be havin' 'olladay fer zix weeks. Whether they'll ever last that long or no I can't say. But if they do I fancy 'twill zeem very leisurable to 'em when they gets back to work. I'll make a bet if they was compelled to work half so hard fer their living as what they do 'olladay-making they'd kick up a purty vine shindy. I reckon 'tis 'most time they had a 'Olladay-makers' Union to stop any of 'em workin' more'n twenty-vower hours a day."

"What do they do then, Mr. Zalter, so much of it?" says Mrs. Endycott.

"I'm darned if I knaw hardly what they do, missis, excep' that they'm on the go all the time. They zeem to have got the idaya that unless they'm rishin' about the whole o' the time they ban't makin' the most o' their 'olladay. Rather than sit still and do nort fer a minute they'll rin upstairs and down again or dap around the taable a time or two. Bevore they'm half-ways through one caper they'm scheming what they can be up to next, so's not to lost no time in between."

"I shude'n think they can scheme very much this weather, poor toads," says Mrs. Snell. "'Tis nothin' but rain every day alike."

"They daun' make very much odds about the rain," says Tom. "They'd sooner get wet right in through to the skeen than they'd bide quiet in-houze and rest a bit. If they've planned to go any-place they'll go, rain or sheen. If they can't go in comfert they'll go in hopes. I never zee'd such people fer hopes in all my born days. If they zees a bit o' blue sky the size of a drip'my-bit that's quite sufficient fer they to prophesy a vine day. It never have'n happened yet, more than about o' twice, but they goes on hopin' all the zame."

"But I thought you said you'd had a day's 'olladay yourself, Mr. Zalter."

"I did say so, Mrs. Snell. At laiste, they said 'twas a day's 'olladay, so I s'pause it must be true; but I shude'n 'a-knowed it if they had'n told me."

"Who do 'ee mean? Your visiters?"

"That's right, missis; the boarders or lodgers or whatever they be. They took me away fer a day's pleasure."

"That was very kind of 'em."

"I dersay they meant it fer kindness. But I 'ope they won't do it again. Well, there, I'll zee they don't.

"They'd schemed out this-yer outin' the night bevore, with maps spread out all over the table, and planned a journey to Bude and Clovelly, and I dunnaw where they wad'n gwain. And then one aw'm, a bit more stoobid than the rest, thought 'twude be a gude idaya to take me along with 'em. They said 'twude do me gude. Why on earth they shude imagine that I wanted doing gude to I can't think, but they'd properly made up their minds that I shude go this trip along wai' 'em.

"Of coorse I laafed it to scorn when they mentioned it to me.

"'Thank 'ee all the zame fer the compliment,' I said, 'but it cude'n be done. There's vorty jobs waitin' fer me to zee to about the place, and I reckon my missis wude have zummin to say if I was to go off gallivantin' all day and leave her to do it all.'

"But I'm bothered if my missus wad'n stood jist outzide the door and yer'd what I said.

" 'Lor massey,' her says to the ladies and gen'lmen, 'he need'n let that stand in the way. I shude be only too thankful to have 'n out o' my way fer a day. I cude get on with twice as much work as I can with he pokin' about.'

" You can jist imagine how they did laaf; and I cude'n very well hatch up another excuse 'pon-tap o' the fust wan. So I had to say I'd go. But I wish I'd knawed that mother was so near. I'll make a bet I'd have had a differ'nt yarn to that.

" They've got two moters, thase people have; one called a two-saiter which holds dree, and one called a vower-saiter which holds vive. So 'twas ordained that young Mr. Charles and his mother shude go in the small car, and the rest of us in the big one; that was the old gen'lman and the two young ladies and me. The orders was that us was to be ready to start by zeb'm 'clock in the mornin' so's to 'low a gude long day; and all the grub us wude require was to be putt up in parcels and packed in the moters, so's us cude ait our meals by the zide o' the road.

" That's another o' the redecklus items belongin' to this-yer 'olladay caper, aitin' yer dinner by the zide o' the road. Lor bless 'ee, when they volks be home, if anybody was to ferget to let 'em have the second vork, or laive the pipper off the table, or putt down a tableclath with a durty spot on it, they'd play 'amlick. Everything mus' be jis' so, else they can't ait nothin', zeem-zo. And yet they'll zit on a sheet o' newspaper in the hedge-traw, with spiders and yerwigs craalin' about, and they'll ait pasties out of a papern bag and drink their tay out of a tinnen cup, and pick up the shugger with their vingers and get the bits of egg-shell mixed up with their braid-an'-butter and call they'm injoyin' theirzels.

"That's becus 'tis 'olladay. If they was forced to do it 'twude be purgatry.

"However, 'twas ordained that us shude start at zeb'm 'clock, so I got ready about of eight, 'cus I've zee'd that zeb'm 'clock caper bevore. The visiters beginned to creep down over the stairs about 'ar-past eight, with all manner of excuses why they had'n got up zooner. By the time they finished brekfas' and all had a knock with their knuckles to my weather-glass till they'd scat all the nature out of 'n, 'twas gone nine, so they started rishin' around and gettin' in each other's way. When they come to take the big car out from the linney they found he'd got a pumsher.

"'It won't take 'ee a minute to putt on the spare wheel,' says the ole lady.

"'That's no gude,' says Mr. Charles, 'cus if us was to have another pumsher on the road us wude'n have no spare wheel. Us'll have to mend this wan.'

" Vine job that was. Us had to take off the wheel, get off the tyre, mend the hole where he was leakin' to and putt 'n on again. It don't sound very much to say it like that, but I'm beggered if us wad'n haivin' and shovin' and puffin' and blawin' fer best part of a nower over thik job. I don't think they'd had very much experience in that line, and o' coorse the ole gen'lman cude'n do very much to it so it come back to Mr. Charles and me. I knowed as much about takin' off a tyre as the pig knows about arithmetic, so what I helped with one hand I hinedered with tother. And you've no idaya what antics a tyre will get up to sooner than go where you wants 'n to.

" Well, and when us got that job settled there was more trouble. You daun' want to go very fur to find trouble if there's moters about, zeem-zo. The li'l car made up his mind he wude'n start ; and nothing they cude do wude'n make 'n to, nuther.

" You zee, us had'n got rume to keep the both cars in under a roof, so they was forced to putt a cover over the li'l one and let 'n lie out. So he'd ketched a cold in the night and his works wude'n go round. I thought 'twas a very gude opportunity fer me to get shut of the whole affair, so I said, ' You'd better-way all get in the big car and laive me behind, and I'll come some other time.'

" But they wude'n have that. I was afraid they wude'n.

" ' Us'll start 'n in a minute,' says Mr. Charles. So he turned the hannle round and round till he was black in the face. Then I had a go at 'n, and I turned till I was all colours o' the rainbow. But not he wude'n start. Once or twice he gived a bit of a cough and spit a time or two, but he finished with the zame. 'Twas jist nuff to make 'ee keep on at it a bit longer than you wude else. And he wad'n aisy turnin', begad. I'd sooner turn mother's mangle fer a week than I'd turn that one fer vive minutes. And o' coorse the women volk kep' on sayin' what time 'twas, and how fur us wude a-bin by now if us had started zeb'm 'clock.

" ' Us won't try no more that way, Tom,' says Mr. Charles, when I cude'n have turned the hannle around once more if anybody had offered me vive shullins. ' I know a better way than that.'

" ' I wish you'd said so bevore,' I thought to mezelf.

" ' Us'll push 'n up top o' the heel,' he says, ' and then he'll start by hiszelf down tother zide.'

" You knows that steep bit of a nap outzide o' my place, daun' 'ee ? Well, that's where us was gwain to push 'n up to. Wan o' the maidens sot up in the sate to turn the guidin' wheel, and us three shoved behind ; that was me and Mr. Charles and the ole gen'lman. I reckon I was shovin' as much as they two putt together. And even then it wad'n a very fast job. Us wude go about a yard and then trig up zummin behind the wheels and blow a bit. I offered to harness in my hosses and haal 'n up, but the ole gen'leman said it wad'n worth while, 'cus us was gettin' on very nice. I dersay us was so-fur as he was consarned, cus he wad'n shovin' hard nuff to push a sprat off a grid-ire. Time us had got thik car up to the haid o' the heel I'd had all the 'olladay I wanted. I'd a-bin very glad to get on with my own work for a rest.

" But they was determined I shude go on injoyin' mezelf, whether I wished or no. The li'l car started all right down the heel, although I was prayin' he wude'n. So Mr. Charles and his mother went off in he, and the rest of us got in the big one. Natcher'ly, I thought the father was gwain to drive, but I'm jiggered if that there Miss Kitty did'n get up and ketch hold to the guidin' wheel. Made me so-nervous as a cat, cus her id'n but a li'l bit of a thing, 'bout of eighteen or nineteen, and if a gurt car like that was to take it into his haid to run away her cude'n hold 'n back fer certin. Her wude'n be able to hold a hand-cart, let alone a gurt moter.

"However, the rest did'n zeem to mind, so I s'pause twad'n my place to complain. They sot me in the back sate 'longzide of Miss Jessie."

"'Is that Miss Jessie I sees in the village, zometimes?' says Ned Annaferd.

"'I dersay 'tis, maister.'

"'Daun' wear no hat, do 'er?'

"'I don't think her do as a rule. Daun' wear sitch a turrable lot of anything, come to that. None of 'em don't, nowadays.'

"'Well, if 'tis the zame young lady that I mean, I don't zee you've got so very much to complain about, Tom.'

"'I ban't grummlin' about that part,' says Tom, 'and I dersay I shude 'a-got along all right, but us had'n bin started more'n about ten minutes bevore it commenced to rain, and it rained off an' on fer the rest o' the day.'

"'You had a cover to the car I s'pause, Tom?'

"'There was a cover to 'en, but they did'n putt 'n up unless it acsh'ly rained like billy-o. They said they did'n want to have up the cover if they cude avoid it, or the hood as they termed it, cus they cude'n view the country proper. 'Tis my belief that when people goes fer 'olladay they takes laive o' their sainses. What, fer gudeness' sake, they wanted to view that country vor I dunnaw. It give me the shivers, with the hay lied about spoilin' all over the place. 'Tis only gwain to be a shower,' they said. ' 'Tis hardly worth-a-while puttin' up the hood.'

" And then they'd zay to me, ' If you'd rather have the hood up, Mr. Zalter, you say so, and us'll stop and putt 'n up.'

" All very vine! I cude'n say, ' Ees, I wants it up,' when they'd jis' said they wanted it down, cude I? But 'twas all very well fer they. The two up in front was protected with the winder, and 'twas comin' in my zide behind, so Miss Jessie wad'n gettin' the full brunt aw't. However, it come lickin' down after a bit so they had to stop and putt up the cover, whether or no.

" ' But us need'n putt up the side curtins,' says Miss Jessie. ' Us won't be able to look out at all, else. What do you say, Mr. Zalter? 'Tis just as you like.'

" What cude I say, when her'd that minute said her did'n want the side curtins? Bezides, I did'n know what sort o' things the side curtins was when they *was* up, so I let it go to that. I knowed it cude only last all day; if it had bin any longer I wude'n 'a-putt up wai't.

" And, of coorse, it makes it very ockerd when

people like that is doing their huttermost to make 'ee injoy yerzelf. You can't say the things you'd like to say, cus you daun' want to hurt their feelin's. If they was doin' it on purpose to punish 'ee, then 'twude be a differ'nt thing. Anybody cude turn around and tell 'em zac'ly what they thought about the 'olladay and they too. But when they'm under the impression they'm givin' of 'ee a trate, and all the time keepin' on shall they do thees, thik and tother? or wude'n you like so-an-so and so-an-so, you can't very well say, 'Aw, fer heaven's bide still and laive me alone and let me have a minute's paice.' 'Twude look like bad behaviour; but that's what you veels like sayin'. I did, anyway. If they had'n all tried to be so nice I cude have said, 'I be cold as a frog, the draft is cuttin' the top of me haid off and I be gettin' roomatics in me shoulder, so jus' you putt up the zide curtins and every other sort o' curtins you've got and then turn around and take me home quick as you can.'

"That's what I cude have said. What I acsh'ly did say, was: 'I be very comferable, thank you.' And a bigger lie never was told. I hope I shall be fergiven fer 't, fer he was told in a gude cause."

"'It daun' make no odds about the cause,' says Mrs. Endycott. 'Lies is lies.'"

"'I wude'n contrydict 'ee, missis,' says Tom, cus 'tis a subjic' you knows a lot more about than what I do.'

"Ned Annaferd said: 'I'm surprised, Tom, that you shude take so much notice o' the weather with such a nice young lady sot bezide 'ee. I shude'n 'a-thought you'd know whether 'twas raining or what it was.'

"'That's very nice to rade about in bukes, maister,' says Tom; 'and 'tis all right fer the young people, I dersay. But so far as I'm consarned, I'd sooner be out with a team of hosses mezelf. I shude feel more at home. What with the noise o' the moter and the weend blowin' in around I cude'n properly grasp what her was tellin' about, so I said "Ees" and "No," and I dersay half the time I said "No" where it shude 'a-bin "Ees," and "Ees" where it ought 'a-bin "No."'

"I was glad as a burd when they told about stoppin' fer lunch. 'Twad'n that I was hungered so much, but I thought if I got zummin inzide o' me 'twude help get me warm. So us drayed in on the bit o' grass bezide the road and waited fer the li'l car to ketch us up, cus us passed he miles back. And jus' cus it did'n happen to be rainin' strames at the time we must all get out and have our grub picnic-fashin' as they called it. Idiotic fashin I calls it, sot about with yer knees under yer chin, a pasty in one hand and a cup o' zummin in tother.

"And to make matters wiss I'm bothered if they did'n try to burn my inzide out at the start. At laiste, I daun' suppose they done it a-purpose, but I wish zomebody had warned me.

"Miss Kitty was powerin' zummin out o' wan o' they vaccum flaskis. 'Have a cup o' zoup, Mr. Zalter,' her says. I said, 'I daun' mind if I do, if you've got a-plenty.' So her fulled up my cup.

"A drop o' zoup was jis' what I veeled like, and the whole lot wad'n much more than one gude mouthful, so I let back most aw't to one gullup.

"My eyes and limbs! I wad'n aware they vaccum flaskis cude hold the yet like that. 'Twas scal'-'ot, min! 'Twas on the very verge o' boilin'. The agony! My dear zaul! I'd a-got a mouthful o' vire! Rid-'ot coals cude'n 'a-bin no differ'nt. I cude'n swaller it. 'Twude 'a-killed me. And I cude'n let it bide where 'twas to. There was only one thing to do and that was to blow it out the way it went in. And there was no time to think about manners or lookin' in the right derection. So they had to share it amongs' 'em. And I wad'n so very sorry, 'cus they shude 'a-told me 'twas too hot to drink.

"But my poor mouthe! All around my lips and all across the top o' me tongue was proper bladders. I had to rayfuse one o' mother's pasties, the only thing they'd got there worth aitin'. I cude'n bear it up agin my lips. The only thing I cude have was zome o' that stoobid old shaky trade; you know, jelly stuff; cus that was cold to the vire in me mouthe. I told 'em I preferred that to aught else, and that was another lie, Mrs. Endycott, I don't mind tellin' 'ee.

"Then it come on to rain again, bucketfuls. So everything had to be putt away quick, and 'twas decided to go straight on to Bude. The li'l car went on ahaid, cus us cude go faster and ketch vore to 'en. Or so they reckoned, but it did'n happen this time. As I told 'ee, our car was in on the grass by the zide o' the road, and I suppose with so much rain the ground had got all sauft, and when Miss Kitty tried to start 'n gwain he never moved a inch. The hine wheels wude go round and round but they wude'n go vore.

"You never zee'd sitch a barney in all your born days as what that was. I've knawed of a cow gettin' in the zugs, but never a moter bevore. Every time Miss Kitty started the works gwain he'd roar like a train in a tunnel and his wheels wude whizz around, but they'd only go deeper in the ground.

" So then us all had to got out in the rain to zee if he'd start without the weight. But not he wude'n. By this time he'd digged proper pits fer hiszelf. They tried puttin' the mats in under the wheels, and broke two butiful mats all abroad to rags. But the ole toad wude'n shift. I thought praps he'd start with a bit of assistance, so I said to Miss Kitty ;

" ' I'll get behind and shove,' I says. ' When I holley, " Right," you do whatever you do's to make 'n go and I'll push.'

" They thought that was splendid idaya. So I got behind and digged me toes in the ground and putt me shoulder down to the car.

" ' Right,' I says. And bevore I had time to shut me mouthe again, up come a strame of mud and muck just as if it had bin shot out of a gun. Some of it I swallered and the rest went all over me . . . in me eyes, down me neck, in me butes, up me nawse. I never pushed a pound, cus I was so took by surprise ; and there was the ole wheels whizzin' around and spurtin' up strames of mud and watter. You never zee'd sitch a state as my best clothes was in ; and the number of times mother warned me to take care of 'em.

" I had another go at pushin' aw'n standin' clear o' the wheels ; but I mid all-so-well try to shift Bellever Tor. And wet droo by this time, mind.

I cude veel little trickles back o' me knees and in under me arms.

" Jis' then Mr. Charles come back with the little car to zee what had happened, and they had a bit o' rope and haaled 'n out.

" When I got back in the moter the place I'd bin keepin' dry and warm was got all puddles o' watter, and cold, and the weend cut in around me like knives. But the rest aw'm zeem to be quite happy to think us was able to travel on again. Laafin' over it they was, as if 'twas a vine joke. But I cude'n zee nothin' very funny about it mezelf.

" However, 'twas got later than they anticipated, so 'twas decided to miss Bude altogether and go straight on to Clovelly. If they'd left it to me I shude 'a-said, 'Muddlecombe, nex' stop.'

" Matter o' fact, us did'n ever get to Clovelly, cus Miss Kitty was drivin' along and volleyin' what her thought was the little car, and twad'n the little car 'tall. 'Twas a differ'nt little car, zac'ly like it. Us volleyed that one fer miles, and got all in the wrong derection. Then us did'n knaw what to do.

" 'Mother will think there's bin a accident, and her and Charles will go back on the road us came, so if us went to Clovelly us wude'n vind 'm.'

" However, us *did* vind 'em, more by luck

than jidgment, jus' as it was comin' in dimsey. So then us had to make our way home-along.

"My gudeness! Wad'n I zome glad to get to bed!

"And the nex' mornin' they axed me if I injoyed the trip.

"'Injoyed it!' I says. 'I never had such a day in all my life bevore.'

"And that time, Mrs. Endycott my dear, I told the truth, if I never tells it again."

3. HAVE WE LIVED BEFORE?

They zay one thing brings up another, and when a body comes to think it over 'tis amazin' what subjic's used to be told about in Tom Zalter's ole carrier's cart on the way into market. Zometimes they was sensible and zometimes they was nonsensible. The laistest remark might turn 'em eether-one o' the ways.

I remember one day Mrs. Snell and Mrs. Endycott was tellin' in the carrier's cart how they'd bin to zee the wile baiste show and what a time they'd had, and how they injoyed theirzels lookin' to all they funny animals and so on and so forth; and Mrs. Cann said, "I fancy you two have bin merry-makin' by the zound aw't, ab'm 'ee?"

"Ees, fai," says Mrs. Snell. "Why shude'n anybody have a bit o' pleasure zometimes. Us be only in the world once, so might as well make the best aw't."

Tom Zalter turned around in his ole-fashin way and said:

"Be you sure o' that, missis?"

"Be I sure o' what? I'm sure o' one thing. That ole baccy-smauk o' yours is 'nuff to chuck anybody. Can't 'ee blow it some other way? 'Tis comin' back yer like burnin' ole garden rummidge. Whatever ole trade do you call you'm smaukin'? 'Tis 'nuff to poison a fitch."

"Daun' you like my baccy, missis? 'Tis very nice baccy. The squire let me have best part of a pound aw't, so you'll have plenty o' time to get used to it. He purchased it cheap fer the gardener to smauk to kill the vlies on his roses."

"A very gude thing fer the purpose I shude think," her says. "No vlies cude'n live through that, I'm very certin."

"Well, 'twas a bit too successful, to tell 'ee the truth," says Tom. "It killed the vlies all right, but all the roses twisted up and daied likewise, and by the end o' the week the squire had lost two dogs, leb'm hens and the li'l maid's pet rabbut. Then the gardener had to be took away to 'ospital, one o' the maids went home bad, and they had to have the doctor in to the rest, and all the grass on the lawn turned yaller. So the Squire said if I mind to accep' the rest o' the baccy I cude have it fer carry'ing away, pervided I did'n smauk it within a gunshot o' the Manor. Us ab'm lost nothin' in our houze up to now, 'seps two cats and the canary-burd, but my missis had'n opened her eyes up to the time I come away 's-morning. . . ."

"Hold thee baal, thee gurt mump'aid," says missis. "I dunnaw which is worse, yer ole baccy-smauk or the twaddle you tells up."

"I'm vexed you don't like the smauk," says Tom, "but you can open the back o' the cart and let the ventilation blow through or you can ride up 'pon top, whichever you mind to, but I can't blow the smauk tother way on account o' the hosses. Hosses is very dillicate craytures in that rispect."

"I like yer manners, Tom Zalter. You regards yer hosses bevore yer passengers, then?"

"Certinly I do, Mrs. Snell. Hosses costs a lot o' money, but I can get passengers fer nothin'."

"Well, I never did! If you ban't a proper gen'lman then I never zee'd one. But what did you mean by sayin', just now, was I sure us was only in this world once? How many times do you think you've bin in it, twice?"

"Well, there, that I can't say, Mrs. Snell. But there is volks a lot cleverer than I be what considers us have bin in the world ever so many times bevore."

"What ever stoobid ole item be you on upon now, fer gudeness' sake? You'm talkin' more daaft than usual 's-morning, and that's needless, upon my word."

"'Tis no items o' mine, missis. I got it from a very larnid man, and Jan there can verify what I say. You remember thik professer chap, Jan, what told up his ole logic into the Ins'ichute? 'Twas the time us had thik 'Serious of Lecshers' when everybody was mazed about Higher Eddication. He made up a long ole yarn all about when us was on earth bevore, thousan's o' years agone. You must remember the feller, Jan, cus I zee'd you screwin' up yer faace and tryin' to make wise you understood what 'twas all about."

"I mind the chap very well," I said, "but I cude'n make tap ner tail o' what he was tellin' about."

"Ner nobody else, neether, I shude think," says Tom. "The bettermost volk was waggin' their haids all the time and pretendin' they was takin' it all 'een, but arter 'twas over the squire and the doctor and the paasen was stood talkin' together, and I noticed their conversation was all about vox-huntin' and not a word of what the perfesser had bin yappin' about."

"What did 'er zay, this-yer perfesser?"

"You've axed me zummat now, Mrs. Snell. There was a lot o' people present owing to a bit of a misunderstanding. When the paasen gived out the notice the week bevore, us thought he said 'twas gwain to be a lecsher on 'Rearin' Carnations.' My missis went on that account cus her's very partial to her bit o' flower-garden. Carnations was very nice flowers, her said, and if there was aught to be picked up about rearin' 'em proper her might-so-well yer it, seein' there wad'n nothin' to pay. And there was sevver'l more went fer the zame raison. But they was had, proper, all the lot aw'm. 'Twad'n 'Rearin' Carnations' the paasen said; 'twas 'Re-incarnation.'"

"And what's that, then?"

"Don't ax silly questions, Mrs. Snell."

"But you yer'd it all, did'n 'ee? So you ought to know."

"You've yer'd your ole stag-turkey gobble many-a-times, ab'm 'ee? But you dunnaw what he's talkin' about. Anyway, this feller never said a word about carnations, ner no other kind o' flowers. All he told was a long ole rigmarole about how us had all lived on this earth bevore, in old ancient times, and arter us be daid and gone us will come back and live all over again.

"Was er mazed, or what?"

"I can't tell 'ee, missis. He did'n appear like anybody mazed, and whether he was mazed or no he was able to spin up a middlin' gude yarn. It all come out so-suant as rinnin' watter; did'n it, Jan?"

"But do you mean to tell me," says Mrs. Snell, "that I shude'n remember if I'd ever been plagued with a feller like you bevore. Anybody wude'n ferget that, not if 'twas a thousand years."

"Half a minute, missis. You ab'm got the idaya, not yet. So fur as I cude understand us wad'n the zame when us was yer bevore as what us be now. Us was in a differ'nt department, in a manner of spaikin'. What I mean to say, us did'n start as human men and women. In they days us was only animals, or praps only creepy-crawlies. And then each time us come back——"

"Aw, us have been back more'n once, have us?"

"To be sure. Us keeps on gwain and comin' back, accordin' to the perfesser. And every time us comes back us goes up a peg or down a peg accordin' as how us got on the time bevore. I can't explain it proper cus 'twas too deep fer my brain to fathom. But s'posin' fer instance a body was a cat, and he was a middlin' gude cat, ketched a-plenty o' mice and did'n go in the larder or keep anybody awake with his zingin' of a night, then nex' time he come back praps he might be a dog. Well, and the nex' time he might be promoted to hoss, fust a gipsy's hoss and go around with cloas-pegs and sweepin' brushes, and the nex' time he might be pullin' the Laurd Mayor's coach. And if he done that proper and did'n juggle the Laurd Mayor about or kick the stable-boy he might be promoted nex' time to be a human man. Then 'twude depend on how he behaved hiszelf what sort o' man he'd be when he come back again nex' time. The fust time he might only be crackin' stoans. But if he gived his mind to his work and cracked the stoans well, he might come back and be a jook or a bishup. He might even be Laurd Mayor o' Lunnon ; and that wude be a funny thing, wude'n it, to be fust of all in the sharps and arterwards inzide the coach ? "

" But s'posin' he did'n do his work proper ? S'posin' he was a rogue and a vagabone and every thing that was bad ? "

" Aw, well, in that case, missis, he'd go back again, and praps the nex' time he'd be a camel and have to go fer days and weeks without a drink and carr' tremenjis gurt loads across the bakin' hot desert. And if he wad'n a gude camel he'd keep on gwain back and back till he got where he started to."

"And what wude that be?"

"Well, missis, from what I cude make out, us was all maggits to begin with and graj'ly worked our way up."

"You nasty, bais'ly thing, you, Tom Zalter. I s'pose you'll say bim-bye that once upon a time I was 'opping about in chayse."

"You can't tell, Mrs. Snell. And jidgin' by the way you jumped last Vridy when you sot down 'pon Mr. Annaferd's roll o' barb wire I shude say 'tid'n 't all unlikely. But if what the perfesser says is right it only shows 'ee how you ought to be kind to animals. Jus' fancy, when you putts the stick about the dog or kicks the cat out droo the dairy winder you might be ill-traitin' yer own gran'mother."

"How can you zit there and tell up sitch a parcel o' trumpery, Tom Zalter?" says Mrs. Endycott. "Don't 'ee incourage the gurt stoobid, Mrs. Snell. 'Tis rale right-down wickedness, and if he id'n careful he'll be struck comical vor 't. Well, there, he's that already. But I reckon he'll be punished vor such pervarsity, and 'twill be wonder to me if zummin draidful don't happen to 'en."

"Well, I dunnaw," says Mrs. Snell. "I

wude'n say but what there's a bit o' truth in it arter all."

"Mrs. Snell! How ever can you say such thing?"

"Well, Mrs. Endycott, don't you remember when us was into the wile-baiste show tother day and lookin' to they there monkeys. If you mind, there was one pa'ticler hugly feller in a cage all by hiszelf, and us remarked at the time what a likeness there was between he and Tom Zalter. Sevver'l people noticed it. I wude'n be 't all surprised if that id'n what Tom was the last time he was on earth, and I shude say by the way he's gwain on, that's what he'll be when he comes back again. Anyway, when us gets to Exeter I be gwain to buy a bag o' nuts in readiness."

4. BREATHING-ROOM ONLY

Although the ole Carrier's Cart is purty well a thing o' the past now, I likes to look back zometimes and remember zome o' the journeys us had, and the volks that was there, and the way us was packed een on speshul occasions which brought along a vew extry passengers, and the jokin' that went on. Ther' wad'n a tremenjis lot o' rume to spare ordnery times, and then if you got half-a-dizzen more 'pon-top o' that you had to sit up middlin' tight together, and lucky to vind a bit o' sate big enough to swear by. 'Twas amazin' how us used to get jus' one more body een arter the ole cart was full up, and then two or dree more arter that.

I mind one trip us had a vortnit bevore Crissmus when us was full up to the start and then keeped on pickin' up fresh passengers on the way. There was alwis a-plenty wanted to go on that journey to view the shops into Exeter and purchase a vew things fer Crissmus and such like.

As I zay, us was packed up purty tight when us left Muddlecombe and then when us got to Lower Aish ole Tom Zalter turned around on his driver's sate and said :

" Yer's ole Luke Shillabeer wantin' to ride in-along. You ab'm got rume inzide there fer the ole feller, have 'ee ? "

" Rume ! " says Mrs. Endycott. " No-ti-no. Us ab'm got rume fer a cat. I've bin tryin' to wipe me nawse fer the last ten minutes and I can't come to me pocket to take out me 'ankcher."

" Well, must I tell the ole gen'lman he must stop behind ? " says Tom. " Crissmus and all."

" Don't 'ee tell 'n no such thing," says Mrs. Snell. " Let the poor ole feller come een. Us'll make a space fer 'n zome'ow. 'Twill help keep us hot. I don't matter how much they squaises me up. The more the better. Mrs. Endycott must go on sniffin', that's all."

And so us wedged in ole Luke zome'ow and the cart was stuffed like a sofa cushin. Mrs. Annaferd said there wad'n rume fer a yer-wig to get in now. And arter that us picked up Susan Caunter to Ridgate and Mrs. Samway's li'l maid to the Quarries. Everybody said us muzzen laive ole Susan behind, zeeing her'd trapesed more'n two mile droo the snow, and there was plenty willin' to let li'l Bessie Samways sit 'pon their lap.

And by that time us was fer all the gude in the world like herrin's in a box. Mrs. Endycott reckoned her cude'n braithe, and Mrs. Snell said 'twas the fust time her'd been hot since her got up out o' bed. Then everybody started to laaf, and cude'n tell no more'n Adam what they was laafin' about. And mind you, once you starts that sort o' laafin' 'tis a job to stop.

And then, I be dal'd, when us come to Gibbet Cross if there wad'n two more stood waitin'; George Webber's wive to Wes'lands and her ole mother, Granny Steevins.

" 'Tis no gude," says one body. " Us won't all get to Exeter alive as 'tis."

So us all bust out laafin'. What on earth there

was to laaf about gudeness only knows, but us had properly got the grizzles by thees time. If one body only said they'd got the peens and niddles everybody else roared laafin' like a parcel o' looneys.

Tom Zalter said, " Well, what be gwain to do about it? Be 'ee gwain to let thase two poor women perish in the snow, like the babbies in the wude?"

Us all laafed again. There wad'n no raison to laaf, but us had got like it. Luke Shillabeer says:

" Mrs. Steevins can zit on my lap if her'll promish not to tell my missis."

When you come to think that Granny Steevins is in her zemp'ty vive you mid depend there was zome merriment over that.

" I'm very willin' to zit on the vloor if you'll let me to," says Mrs. Webber."

" On the vloor!" says Ned Annaferd. " Laur bless yer zaul, us ab'm zee'd the vloor since us left Orcombe Cross."

" Only thing to do is to make a heap at the back," says Tom Zalter, " and stack 'em up one tap tother." So o' cou'se us had another gude laaf over that.

But I'm bothered if that id'n purty nearly what it come to. Tell about sheep in a pen! They was a king to what we was.

Lias Buzzacott said, " I reckon the Inspecter

of Cruelty to Animals ought to come and take Tom Zalter's name and derections."

Us cude yer Lias's voice but us cude'n zee 'en. He was buried zomewhere up the var end. But he keeped on makin' his stoobid remarks.

"Can 'ee zee a leg pokin' out there anywhere belongin' to me, Mr. Shillabeer?" he said. "I can't vind but the one, and I had two when I got een. I know I had, cus I used 'em both this mornin'."

"I can't say, hardly, Lias," says Luke. "There's sevver'l yer, all shapes and sizes, but I dunnaw whether you belongs to eether-one of 'em or no."

"Well, I wish you'd pinch 'em one to a time, maister, and I'll tell 'ee if you comes to mine."

"You'd better not go pinchin' mine," says Mrs. Endycott. "I'll let 'ee know it if you do."

"That's all right, Luke," says Lias. "You'll know Mrs. Endycott's: hers is the one with the hole in the stockin'."

Aw, my dear days! The vat was in the vire tho. Mrs. Endycott ab'm got much patience with Lias Buzzacott the best o' times, and fer he to say such thing as that about her was like a rid rag to a bull.

"If I cude get at thee I'd give thee a gude scat, thee gurt mump'aid."

"Ah! But you can't get at me. I can't get

at mezelf even—not without movin' half the parish."

"I shall have 'ee fer that piece o' chick, zooner or later, you lyin' ozeburd. And when I do I'll give 'ee what you'm askin' vor."

"Never mind, missis," says Lias, from in under his load, "I be gwain to buy two-pennerd o' misseltoe when us gets into Exeter if I'm still livin', and then us can make it up gwain home-along in a proper manner."

My hyvers! How us did laaf to be sure.

"You sassy toad, you," says missis. "If I cude only free my arm I'd give thee a scat across the haid with Mr. Annaferd's walkin' stick, I wude, to larn 'ee behaviour."

"Laur bless 'ee, Mrs. Endycott," says Mrs. Snell, "you'd need zummin differ'nt to a walkin' stick to larn Lias behaviour. A stonen gate-paust wude be more suitin' his thick haid."

Lias laafed so-much as anybody. "Who's gwain to pay fer the brocken gate-paust?" he said.

Not even a wumman can get the last word with Lias, and that's sayin' zummat, begad.

You can imagine what 'twas like gwain back home-along, arter everybody had bin purchasin' their Crissmus things into the shops. To zee the volks and the parcels outzide the cart bevore us started you'd say 'twas impossible to get 'em all een. And I'm middlin' sure no other body but Tom Zalter cude 'a-done it. But he managed it zome'ow, and the only thing you cude say about it, was, 'twas before walkin' all they miles. Still, you was very thankful when the fust lot o' passengers got out and gived 'ee braithing rume.

Lias Buzzacott was buried back behind again, and every wips-wile us yer'd his voice comin' out o' the dark.

" 'Tis hard to die so young," he said. "I knawed they was wrong when they said I was born to be hanged, but I did'n think I shude have to be stiffled to death. 'Tis a 'orrible death, stifflication."

And bim-bye he said again in a li'l smaal voice as if 'twas his last words :

" I did hope I shude be spared over Crissmus, but I s'pause it wad'n to be. Tell Tom Zalter I fergives 'en the ninepence he never paid me fer mendin' his harness twelve month agone last Lady Day."

'Twas hawful fulishness, when anybody comes to tell it over, and I suppose us ought to be glad that they days has passed away. Us rides in a moter now, with strangers from other parrishes, so us sits up and behaves ourzels, and says 'tis very nice weather but us thinks 'tis gwain to rain bevore the day's out. There id'n time to say very much more cus us flips into market in quarter the time us used to take behind Tom Zalter's hosses.

But I dunnaw. The old way was slow, and very cold zometimes, and turrable tayjis if you was in a hurry. But then, you wad'n alwis in a hurry, and 'twas mortle sociable.

THE END